MISTRESS

WITHIN

ISBN: 978-0-578-42883-3

Dedication

TO GOD OUR FATHER,
JESUS CHRIST AND THE HOLY SPIRIT.

To my sister Nicole King who passed away 12/19/2003.

Finally, my husband, daughter, grandson, my mom and dad, my niece, and great nephew.

MISTRESS WITHIN

By: Sabrina Haynes

Chapters

Foreword

Sabrina and I became acquaintances in the 90s. I then became her hairstylist. During that time, we developed our great friendship; a friendship that has flourished into us working together in ministry. Sabrina is strong, giving, caring, smart and kindhearted. She is committed to loving and serving others. I have witnessed the growth in Sabrina's life spiritually, personally, and professionally. In her commitment to humanity, Sabrina gives her time, talent and treasures unselfishly. She supports, motivates and encourages others to fulfill their purpose in life. Sabrina is a wife, daughter, mother, aunt, grandmother and an Evangelist. Her faithfulness to the Kingdom and her family evidence that Sabrina is a child of the Most-High God. Her light is shining so bring men to see her good works and Glorify the Father in Heaven (Matt 5:16). She is a giver and God is giving back to her pressed down, shaken together and running over (Luke 6:38).

But as it is written, Eye hath not seen, nor ear heard, neither have entered into the heart of man, the things which God hath prepared for Sabrina (1Cor 2:9). *Mistress Within* will be a best seller. This book will free up broken women and men and help them free up others. *Mistress Within* is an Inner Healing tool to Freedom

-Minister Nedra Butler

Introduction

"I can't believe I got myself into this again! Karmah, you must do better. Why can't I get past Denim's sex? Lord I find myself in this situation over and over. My mind keeps thinking of how he caresses my body. His soft lips and minty breath touch my lips. His tongue sweeps across my neck.

He has me again in the bed. His medium-height sexy-built body stands behind me. He gently rubs me from the back and I can't stop him. I give it all to him like I know he loves it...

I just didn't see myself here again. Lord I keep thinking you left me, but I came to the realization I have left you. Take me back to when I was so deep into you...

God I need you."

Karmah was a mistress in all sorts of ways. She slept with several married men. She lusted after men with her eyes and thoughts. Her phone held pictures awaiting the eyes of married men. Karmah couldn't keep her hands off them, and the harder they were to get, the better.

But Karmah wanted to be free. She prayed and cried out to GOD for help laboring at the altar many times for the same sin. There was a war going on inside her.

Denim wasn't her only man, he was simply the one who broke her down and brought out things in her she never could imagine. But because of his actions, she gave God her all. Did Karmah go back to DENIM?

What are those hidden things in you that you're battling with? Understand there is no covering it up! God sees those text messages, hears those phone calls and sees us in action. People of God allow God to clean you up for His glory.

What are you hiding?

In The Beginning

KARMAH was a little girl with she was short, and very slim with full-size lips and dark brown eyes. She wasn't often considered the happiest child. She grew up thinking she wasn't the prettiest girl. Imagine that, I know there are a lot of people that feel that way. Let's go into the mindset of this little girl who went from innocent and saved to SOUL SNATCHER! What is it like for someone like Karmah, a person who has fallen, to find their way back to God? Let's see what people and things could have caused her to be the way she was in her darkest times.

Growing up, she would often hear her family arguing. In her little, terrified mind, she would put her tiny fingers over her ears, close her eyes and hide on the side of the bed hoping to take away the sounds she was hearing. Her older sister would just stand there. Neither of them knew what to do.

She wasn't always happy in the home due to the arguing and fighting. No matter what, she loved her parents unconditionally.

Karmah would later live up to her name! she witnessed lying and cheating in relationships and adultery among married folk. One night, she found a tape of someone being caught in the act of cheating. She remembers a lady from the church flirting with one of her married family members.

Karmah couldn't remember a man who was faithful to his significant other in her life. She grew up thinking every man was bound to cheat so she says to her little undeveloped mind, "I'm going to beat them cheating because they going to cheat anyways." With every man Karmah involved herself with, she would end up cheating on them. Imagine this poor, little girl only knowing how to live one way. She had no way of knowing later down the road, her actions and habits would cause her heartache, pain, soul-ties, mood swings, having a lying tongue and so many other issues.

As we go into the life and mindset of this innocent little girl, ask yourself, "Is this Me as well?" Did you have any similarities growing up or did you even know someone that went through the same thing? Time after time we see issues in the lives of little boys and girls. We must remember when bringing children in the world to be mindful of our actions around them.

In life Karmah took some wrong turns and made decisions she would later have to face. She became engulfed in different confusing emotions and spiritual warfare. She found herself in bondage from sex. But as she got closer to God and became more involved in the church, she learned about soulties. She learned how they are activated and how different things can cause a soultie. As she connected with different men, she noticed emotions and reactions that she would experience or act out. When she thought about the event, she felt it wasn't always "her." Turns out, It was those little demon soldiers attached onto the inside of her.

She had to throw gifts away also. Whatever someone gave her that would remind her of them or just given to her period, she would throw it away because she had to release them from her.

What was on the inside of her would manifest when she was in the bedroom. It was like a monster had grown on the inside of her. Sometimes she couldn't be satisfied even when she was being sexed like she wanted, loved to be sexed. She would say to them, "Choke me! Do it harder, harder, harder..." then if it wasn't to her standards, she would begin to use profanity to get her point across

At the age of fourteen, she lost her virginity to someone much older than she was. He was in high school, a famous basketball player. She went in not knowing she was going to be the star on his court, even more, she became the home team. They would often meet up at his house. To get there without raising suspicion, she would often lie about where she was going. Trips to the movies and to the mall with friends turned into evening hookups.

Sex with him wasn't like some people said. It felt weird to her, but she still tried it again with him. The relationship eventually ended and birthed the monster that would grow on the inside of her. She developed skills in that relationship to make a man crave her and think about her constantly. Sometimes she would even fake orgasms just to make them feel they were doing something.

Then at the age of fifteen she had just started her first job with a real check! One day, she was working front register when these loud-mouth people came in and one of the guys was flirting with her. He was extremely loud with big, pretty white teeth. He had "Manipulator" written all over him but at the time her inexperienced eyes couldn't see it. She could see the way he commanded the attention of other women without effort and how his eyes became fixed on hers. She was behind the cash register blushing. She didn't feel like she was pretty. She was shy and never really thought of herself as even approaching womanhood really, but she continued to smile at this grown twenty-one-year-old man who should have known better. After ordering their food, the group left just as loud as they came in.

Karmah was off for two days. When she returned to work, her coworker Abbie had news for her.

"A man has come in here twice for you."

"For real?!? When's the last time you seen him?" Karmah was genuinely surprised that a person would care enough to check for her.

"Yes girl" Abbie said, "and he was cute with a big smile!"

Karmah struggled to get back to work, trying to look serious while her mind raced over who this "man" could be.

In the blink of an eye as Karmah was looking and talking to another coworker, Abbie sidled up to Karmah.

"There he is!" Abbie said from the side of her mouth.

Karmah turned with a puzzled look. It was the loud-mouthed older man. He had the biggest smile ever, somehow larger than she remembered. Karmah walked over to the counter. They talked briefly, and exchanged numbers. Karmah was in for the roller coaster ride of her life, she did not know what she was getting herself into. The relationship would go on for a while and put Karmah through the wringer.

Karmah was young and naïve. Blaze grew large in her heart. He gained Karmah's trust and eased her into his ways. It did not take long for unexpected attention and gifts to prove that she was always on Blaze's mind.

Soon Blaze would cover Karmah with affection, attention and sex on such a regular basis that any lapse in either could be felt in the center of her chest. Karmah would ask Blaze what was wrong and he would reluctantly offer a sad story.

"My sister told me I have to cover our mother's light bill. I mean, I got it for her lights, but then my lights might not be on in a week..."

"Don't worry about that! I can cover half of your bill. That's enough to keep them on for now right?"

Karmah never imagined Blaze would tell a lie to get a new fit for the weekend or spending money for a road trip with his crew.

Blaze was careful to keep Karmah naïve while having his way with her emotionally. When the "emergency" scam wasn't enough to prove he had her where he wanted her, Blaze would pour gas on her flames of rage by asking her out to event past her curfew. When Karmah declined because she couldn't be out so late, Blaze would suggest taking someone else and at times, ride by her house with women Karmah didn't know in his car.

Karmah would be driven crazy with jealousy, eventually developing a habit of sneaking out of her house to be with Blaze.

During the relationship, she experienced heartache, misery, lies and so many other things. she really loved this loud-mouthed popular guy Blaze, and he loved her.

As she was in high school, she could have focused more but rumors of Blaze's escapades stole her attention. She would hear of other girls he was sleeping around with.

"I'm sure the older girls are laughing at me. It'd be easier if I didn't feel like such a fool." Karmah couldn't quiet her mind. He even took her to her high school prom, where she had to go off on him there. It was like the whole school stopped to hear her yelling and crying, only to see them leave together arm-in-arm.

After prom, it got real. They went to their room. She wanted him to get her pregnant and he granted her wish. The next day, they went to the beach where all the kids would go after prom. She found out she was pregnant at 6 weeks when she got very sick and her mom took her to the ER. They were waiting for what seemed like hours in the room for a doctor. Turns out the results were in.

Blaze couldn't have been happier to hear the news. He always wanted as many babies as he could have. He was there with her through her pregnancy but he became a little more controlling and abusive. When she was pregnant, he gave her a black eye. He swore it was because he didn't know where she was. She figured he was worried she would catch him out with another woman. He was seeing at least six other women she was sure of.

Months later, she had a beautiful daughter at the age of 18. Long after they broke up, he ended up with one of the other women, Trixie, he was using during their relationship. Within his relationship with Trixie, he would still want to have sex with Karmah. So on occasion, Karmah set it up so his new girlfriend could find Blaze in her bed.

Karmah befriended Trixie and even allowed her access to the house. One day, Trixie entered Karmah's home thinking she was picking up clothes Karmah had found for her. Little did Blaze know what was in store for him. As she entered Karmah's bedroom, the look on his face was as if Trixie caught him on top of Karmah. Trixie held back tears but said nothing. She then ran out of the house and down the stairs. Blaze didn't leave. He knew he had them both. Trixie still stayed with him even after what she had seen. She was naïve as well.

Karmah was young and in love with a man who showed he cared about her. But he was a Narcissist as well. He wanted the world to know him and he was all about partying, sex and women. All the women loved him. Some thought Karmah didn't know they were sleeping with him, but she knew. She just was nonchalant about it. Sometimes she really didn't know how to feel. Long after their break-up, she would have sex with different people. She dated a few drug dealers (nothing serious) who had plenty of women as well. She just loved men with the gold who were rough and tough.

What she didn't know about at that time was the word "SOULTIES." What was in them was now a part of her. There was no telling what type of women they came in contact with before her. Now she is battling with a sex addiction and all types of spirits running around in her body. She started looking at other men in Blaze's hometown, she even let a couple of them hit it just to do something. she didn't really enjoy it. She was just living the life as if it was normal.

She got to the point in her life where she would see a man and imagine what their sex was like. Karmah could sex a man with her eyes; just by looking at him. She also developed an attraction to a certain type of Caucasian man. She was lost in her own world of lust and sex games. As you read about Karmah and her different love-schemes, you will see how she came contaminated with different spirits.

Russian Roulette

Karmah would often hang with her guy cousins and, of course, that leads to their guy friends wanting to flirt. She was always on the prowl for her next victim, she began to feel that she was untouchable and she could get whatever man she wanted.

She started seeing one guy named Ghost (a friend of her cousin.) He was very different than her usual lovers and she found that most interesting. He smoked that good stuff often and was the most reserved of his friends. She knew he was married they had a beautiful, loving family. His wife Bree was more on the homely, sweet side. She was surely wife-material but could get hostile if need-be. She dressed very professionally for her job and was always well put-together. But Karmah was not intimidated by her or anyone else. She was out to get whatever pleased her and met her needs, whether sexually or financially. Ghost's occupation caused for him to be in a setting at his home. Karmah found him and his freedom appetizing. She even often conversed with Bree the wife because they would sometime be in the same room at Ghost and Bree's home. Karmah was trifling for real. Karmah eventually went to their home in the beginning for product and services.

Months later Karmah would help him with his business. This eventually led them to them having sex at the home before clients would come. On days when Bree would have worked an eight-hour shift, she would come home and Karmah would still be there. Bree would come in the room where Karmah was at and speak to her and see how she was doing. Ghost made lots of money and he made sure the kids were taken care of as well. Often, he would leave work and meet up with Karmah to get them a hotel, make love to her and spend time with her. They began to play house and he would need reminding that had to get back home to his "other wife." Karmah would be at his home the next morning with the same routine. She wasn't in a relationship, but she felt he was her man. He took care of her like she was the main chick.

One morning Karmah had to go over and help him out and the lady of the house was home.

"Hello. How are you doing?" Bree asked with a cute smile on her face.

"I'm great, how are you?" Karmah asked with a smile and looking at her up and down. She was trying to see what he liked about her. Bree she was a pretty lady who dressed classily, but when they say opposite attract… that sure was the case in their relationship. Bree gathered up their kids and eventually left. Ghost and Karmah wasted no time, they would hug, laugh and then, kiss. They started having sex in the living room like they hadn't seen each other in years. She often would give him special treatment.

On a day she didn't have to work, he told her to come by but park two streets away. She parked her car and began a brisk walk to his house. She heard an argument coming from the house. She continued to go over because he didn't say not to come. She walked up the driveway peeking inside to see who he is arguing with. He was on the speakerphone with Bree. It sounded as if she was home.

She pulled him to the entryway and gave him a hug and kiss while he was on the phone with his wife. She then touched him to get him all riled up. His voice betrayed him as he made a sound without thinking.

"What are you doing? Are you even listening?" Bree asked with concern in her voice

"Nothing, Let me call you back."

Bree noticed the next-door neighbor's curtain move so she told Ghost.

"That's an older couple. They cool."

They proceeded into the house but as soon as Karmah went in and Ghost sauntered back into the entryway, Bree pulled into the yard deranged.

"Go hide in the bathroom downstairs under the cabinet!" Karmah did what he said. Ghost had Bree take him to the store where he texted Karmah telling her to get out of the house as soon as they pulled away. She texted him while outside telling him she does not have a good feeling about being in the house especially with the next-door neighbors' curtain moving. When Karmah got no response, she decided to snoop around in their home waiting for the phone to buzz. Before Karmah realized, twelve minutes had passed. She scrambled to get ready to leave when they pulled up. She hurried to text him but there was no response. Left with no choices, she sprinted back to the bathroom and hiding under the cabinet.

Bree and Ghost come in the house and he still has not responded to Karmah. She just can't understand why. Karmah hears Bree say her name. Bree is telling Ghost she doesn't trust Karmah.

"She wears her tight little clothes over here… she looks sneaky!" Bree is still smoldering.

"I'm not gonna tell you again, she can wear what she wants, I'm only interested in what's under these clothes…" Ghost motioned to Bree grazing her figure with his fingertips.

With those words, her anger melted away. Ghost grabbed Bree and Karmah could soon hear them having sex. She continued to text but he was not replying. Karmah became furious and felt hopeless as she waited for a good moment to finally sneak out.

After a couple hours, Ghost saw her texts and went in the bathroom to get her out.

"Why didn't you leave when I told you to?" Ghost said in hushed tones.

"The neighbor was being nosy…"

"She is getting ready to leave. I will come get you." Karmah heard a bit of rustling and then quiet. Five minutes later, he came and helped her out of the house. As Karmah left, she peeked around the house. Bree's close friend would have spotted her if Karmah wasn't careful. She hurried to her car and sped off

Karmah got plenty infusions of cash from Ghost and on the regular. He made good money and took care of her needs. The relationship lasted a short time. This was Karmah's first encounter with a man known to be married. Karmah would eventually run her mouth to her friends. She thought she could talk about it and they wouldn't put her business out there but soon enough, the word was in the streets. Karmah felt horrible. She didn't want to be labeled a home-wrecker but the city she lived in showed no mercy. Ghost and Bree ended up separating and things soon started falling apart between Karmah and Ghost as well. He started working in a different city. Some nights he would stop by Karmah's house and would have sex, but it wasn't the same. Their conversations started getting shorter and soon after, the sex stopped. Karmah and Bree came face-to-face one day. They had a few words but never touched each other. It could have really gotten ugly because Bree was the fighting type and so was Karmah. Karmah's feelings for Ghost faded even further over time.

Karmah was with Ghost for a time but eventually started hearing Ghost was sleeping around with another woman. She did question him but, of course, he lied and denied. She was also working for him so Karmah knew right then what could possibly be going on… she had been in that same situation. At that point she didn't care what he was doing because she was more focused on what the streets were saying about how she broke up their marriage. She felt horrible on the inside. When she went out to places and she saw people looking at her, she wondered did they know what had happened. God has a way of bringing you out of things. I'm sure Bree questioned him when he could no longer deny the truth and asked questions like: Why did it have to happen? Did you have sex with her in our home? Did you like her sex? Did you give her money? How could you destroy our family?

Karmah was still very young and trying to find herself. Emotionally, she could not have been too happy because if she knew her worth she would have not been with someone else's spouse. She was proving to be very sneaky and deceitful. Just looking for love.

Some people who were also talking about her were her friends. She eventually stopped being around them. Now she must face all the drama, sarcasm, name-calling and whatever else was about to come her way. Grace and Mercy would be with her through it.

Psalm 17:8

Keep me as the apple of the eye, hide me under the shadow of thy wings

Examine The Inner You

Think back on your child hood. What do you feel you lacked most?

What did you see growing up that stuck in your head? It could've been displeasing and caused you to treat people the way you do.

If you had more than one boyfriend/man at a time what do you feel you lacked from your main man that the others gave you?

What craving on the inside did you desire that you no longer want?

Seek counseling if you often feel, "Why do I watch certain things? Why do I do certain things? -or- I really need help."

What causes you not to trust an individual?

Who are you?

What do you love about yourself?

What do you dislike about yourself?

What's causing you pain as of this day?

What makes you happy?

What brings you joy?

What makes you sad?

What makes you angry?

Who hurt you?

How are you going to come out of the things holding you in bondage?

We must Fast and pray

Don't let sin govern you. Lust is danger, it's false advertisement.

He Loves Me For Real

Months later, Karmah meets Ryder, this gentleman who sweeps her off her feet. He has a nice car and a great job. They began dating and things are going great when Karmah realizes she is still battling with demons on the inside of her. She feel like she has to cheat on a man even if the man was a good man. She would still cheat because of her state-of-mind. Her spirit is tapped into the mind-frame that she doesn't know or understand the meaning of being faithful to one man. When she sees other nice-looking men, Karmah undresses them with her wandering eyes. If the man has a woman with them, she just tries to conduct herself more secretly. She imagines what their sex would be like and what size they are as she stares at them from head-to-toe. She imagines them on top of her or her riding them. She must get help from this generational curse that's on the inside of her. She can quickly recall the word that has already been embedded on the inside of her. The issue is so many sex partners she has had, some married, some with girlfriends and just people she has dated. She can feel strange desires from this direction and that inside her thoughts and emotions

Karmah is now getting to know this great guy but she's accustomed to men only sexing her. She can't believe how good she has it with this guy and learns to enjoy being pursued as a whole person. She was very suspicious of him in the beginning. She would play immature games just to see if he would cheat with someone else. He treated her like a lady should be treated but she was stuck on the men that just wanted to beat her back in. Soon her other side would come out. The anger and rage would rise when she heard old stories about his past relationships. She wanted to be the best every man had. A man coming to her with memories concerning relationships, you may suddenly find himself missing some teeth!

Karmah also had an abusive side to her. Growing up she was witness to mental and physical abuse. Depending on her timing, you might have gotten the physical and mental abuse side of her. She even saw Ryder had a soft side to him. That was very different for her. He truly treated her like a queen. Later in a relationship, she started to get more controlling. Karmah found herself demanding to know his whereabouts constantly. Ryder was attracted to her ways but he didn't always put up with her mess.

He would threaten to leave her, but she would always say she didn't mean to act out the way she did.

Soon she would start following him to see where he would be going. She even waited for him to get off work and followed him to Orlando in heavy traffic. He would eventually notice someone following him and he noticed it was Karmah. He played right along with her games and would go from lane-to-lane, weaving through traffic so quickly that she couldn't keep up with him. His Mustang had acceleration that she couldn't muster in a little Nissan.

Her phone rings and Ryder flashes across the screen.

"Hello." says Karmah.

"Hello. How are you? WHERE are you?" Ryder asks knowingly.

Karmah lies, "I'm in the car with my friend… umm we on our way to the hair store."

"Yeah… Okay." mutters Ryder.

She was her biggest enemy. Specifically, what laid dormant on the inside of her. But God had help on the way. She would meet a Christian lady who would lead her back to the church.

Have you had a person who showed you love but you didn't know how do show it back?

Have you been in a situation where you were torn between multiple lovers?

What have you done to get out your situation or are you comfortable in it?

Do you feel you are not good enough for someone?

Why don't you think you are beautiful?

Do you know everything God made was beautiful?

Have you asked God to send you some help?

Seek God in all things and he will direct your paths.

Have you asked God to lead and guide you?

Have you given God a for real YES and really meant it?

Hurt, Deceit and Trauma

In the midst of all her proclivities Karmah hurt people. She was deceitful and in the midst her heart, she held trauma. God is the healer of all things. In the end, all she could do was tell him thank you. Have you ever found yourself in a love triangle and felt there was no way out? Do you know God is the way out? She started to talk to God more and He knows she was tired. God had to deliver her so she could bring someone else out. He never left her, she left Him. He was just waiting on Karmah to surrender it all to Him.

Have you found yourself going through life and you were tired of living a lie? You could've felt like you were all alone and that no one could help you. Maybe you felt that if you confided in someone, they would judge you. Well, yes that could also happen but we have to realize in life that holding all of what we went through or are going to go through can hurt us. We need to release and get prayer, direction, guidance and deliverance.

Look in the life of Karmah. She went on this way for years and years living different lives. Yes, we say God already knows what we are going to go through, but some people don't always see things like that. They want to judge and not empathize with what a person has gone through. That is why people keep their mouths closed and live in a shell for years screaming on the inside. Don't let that be you. Talk to someone even if it's a stranger that does not know your situation.

Often Karmah would be fearful of what would happen to her if she didn't stop what was doing. If you are in a situation and you know it is not right, have you had the same thought? Or do you just think you are untouchable? Think about those questions.

Write a Letter to God and tell him all about it

_____

_____

_____

_____

_____

_____

_____

_____

SIGNED:

Pastor Grey's

CHURCH MISTRESS

"I love Him. I love his touch. I love the warmth of his hands." Karmah recalls.

His lips are silky smooth. When he touches her hips, it's like a vibration goes through her. His eyes are so sexy. His exotic touch makes her back warm. As he kisses her face with his silky-smooth lips, Chills go through her body. she wants to stop spiritually, but her flesh overtakes her.

Thoughts go through her mind, "What am I doing here? We should not be doing this in this place. This is a sacred place for Gods people to come and be delivered. Surely this is not a place to contaminate."

He turns her around on his office desk. His hands glide up her dress. She moans but only for a moment. She wants it, but then again, it's not right. She hears his belt buckle release, then his zipper going down. She hears his pants drop and the next thing she knows, he has inserted himself in her right in the church house. With his hands on her shoulders he pushes in and out of her slowly, slowly, slowly.

He whispers in her ear, "I love you. I never stop thinking about you. Don't leave me baby."

She grabs the desk with her nails so hard that the middle fingernail breaks. His strokes get faster and faster as he bites her neck. He is stroking faster, faster, faster and faster.

She says, "Stop! Stop, someone is coming."

He continues to stroke faster grabbing her harder until... He ejaculates. When he's finished, his body lay over her as if he was motionless.

"Father forgive me..." he groans in resignation.

Now in Karmah's head she's thinking, "Why would he now say Father forgive me? Why would he even want us to do this in God's house?"

A single knock at the door was the secretary, Chelsea, from the connecting room. He jumps up, pulls up his pants, and buckles his belt. Karmah notices he did not zip up his pants.

" Baby are you in there? why is the door locked? Are you asleep?" Chelsea batters the door with questions.

"I'm not." he finally opens the door and says, "Hi Chelsea. How are you?"

She goes up to him, hugs and says, "I'm fine. Baby how are you?" Chelsea looks over to see Karmah standing there. The look on Chelsea's face gave everything away.

"Hi Karmah! That's just a little joke I tell him every now and then, nothing serious.

"Oh I didn't think nothing of it. I put nothing past no one not even your Pastor."

Pastor Grey sensing a rise in tension says, "We are not going to start this. We already had a previous altercation in this church before. Now what just happened will not go outside this door."

Chelsea and Karmah stare at one another, Karmah grabs her purse and walks towards the exit. She plans on leaving the door open. Chelsea's eyes trail to the floor where she finds her next card to play.

"Oh, you forgot something on the floor, Karmah."

But Karmah continues to walk away from the office. Chelsea quickly stoops down, gathers her trump card and hurls it at Karmah.

"I told you there was something you left behind," Chelsea brims with pride as a pair of slinky panties fall at Karmah's feet. "That's rather classless that you can't tell you're leaving them."

Assuming her conquest over Karmah, Chelsea turns toward a clearly upset Pastor Grey.

Karmah, turning around says, "No sister Chelsea, those are not mine." She then pulls up her dress displaying the white lace panties she has on to the pair. "They aren't my style either."

Chelsea says angrily, "So now we see that there have been others in Pastor Grey's office. So Pastor, by me being the secretary, I will be calling a meeting with the members to see how we are going to handle this." Her jealousy is leaking through. "I also noticed your pants were unzipped and I saw you beating Karmah's back in. I think you should have someone fix the little hole in the middle of your door with a magnifying glass. You can see a lot."

Karmah got in her candy red new Porsche and sped off.

"You are so nasty! How could you have sex with both of us in the same day within hours apart? Chelsea's rage is palpable.

"Never question me or I will pull your title as secretary and Evangelist!" Pastor Grey roars just enough to shake her confidence.

"Evangelist?!?" Chelsea turns away, "I am not an Evangelist and if I was, I sure haven't been doing anything for you to even call me that." Pastor Grey tells her, "You stick with me, you will be one. I can do a lot for you if you just keep your mouth shut."

She says not a word.

"Do you hear me?" Pastor Grey rumbles.

Chelsea breathes, then responds, "Do you not know who you are messing with? You don't want to cross me. I will make your life a living testimony of how you went from Cheating Pastor to a sold-out for Jesus Pastor. I will do things to you so tortuous that you will have no choice but to call on Jesus. Now let's get to the reason I came by; did you forget to pay my car payment? The finance people are calling me, and I refuse to answer."

"I'm not paying for your car anymore. Not after I caught you with Deacon Shine at the restaurant. All cash access has been denied to you."

"I already told you, Deacon Shine was helping me with a conference I'm thinking about putting together." Chelsea says on the verge of tears.

"I'm done now do what you have to do, It's over. You don't come in my office threatening me."

Chelsea walks out with a look of revenge.

Karmah exit was largely for show. She was right around the corner from the church waiting for Chelsea to leave. Karmah looks through her binoculars and sees a car pull out of the church exactly like hers. She notices it's Chelsea. But Pastor Grey is now paying Karmah car payment instead of Chelsea. Karmah zooms down the road to approach and stop her.

Chelsea stops, "Ugh now how we end up with the same car? Hey Karmah, have you washed up since leaving Grey's office?"

"Why would I need a bath?"

"Well, like I told Grey, I saw him beating your back in. There is a hole in the door. If you have a magnifying glass, you will see more than you can handle."

"Why do you call him Grey?" Karmah asks.

"I call him Grey because when he has me in the same position he had you, I don't feel comfortable saying Pastor. So I call him Grey."

"And what makes you so comfortable to tell me about you and him?"

"Well God is going to expose it anyways…" Chelsea leans on her Porsche. "And plus he stopped paying my car payment so I'm going to expose everything. It doesn't take a genius to see he's paying your car payment."

"He's going to pay it until it's paid in full." Karmah's phone rings, it's Pastor Grey. She sends him to voicemail. Karmah continues to talk to Chelsea because now they are both being played.

Never play with a woman's heart. Some women can't take that and when your heart is truly in it, danger is about to happen. You never know what that woman has been through in previous relationships, or what happens in a person's childhood. These things point directly to why men do the things they do. A man could have been so hurt that he hid all the hurt and pain never dealing with it. Now he will just play all women, even the ones who truly love him.

First Lady Grey is this sophisticated looking woman who cooks, cleans, washes, rubs his feet and massages his body. She keeps their eight bedrooms spotless. He always calls before he comes home so she can have the jacuzzi ready for him in the room with all glass low hanging lights. She will even have the most soothing music playing.

"Baby I'm on the way home."

First Lady Diamond is her name. She replies, "I will have everything prepared for you."

He gets home within the next 20 minutes. She is at the door waiting on him to take his briefcase and remove his shoes.

She undresses him and mentions, "I see you've been with someone today. I smell perfume on you. Was it Chelsea or Karmah? I'm sick of this. All I do for you and you continue to treat me like trash?"

"When I met you, you were nothing but a stripper. I own you. You have not had to work in over 20 years so never question what I do."

"So, you think I'm going to continue to sit in church and let these whores smile in my face? I don't think so." Diamond thinks. She knows better than to say too much.

This First Lady had been saving up to leave him. She was tired of feeling like a fool and unloved. She started back stripping on the weekends and even began sleeping with some clients. He couldn't care enough to realize this has been going on for three years.

Secrets are deadly depending on the mindset of each person and especially the person dealing the cards.

"So, you think you can survive without me?" says Pastor Grey. Diamond says, "Time will tell... Your water is ready, pajamas are on the bed and dinner will be on the table when you're done."

Karmah sees Pastor Grey left a message when he called her while she was with Chelsea. His message says, "Hello beautiful, I have no Idea whose panties those were. Give me a call."

Karmah calls him but he didn't answer because his phone was on the bed and he was in the Jacuzzi. She continues to call. Diamond walks in from the kitchen and sees Karmah's name come up on the phone.

She says out loud, "He has the nerve to have her name in his phone as her real name?" She's had it! Diamond answers and says, "Karmah, he is in the jacuzzi and I also let him know I am aware of you and Chelsea sleeping with him. So, call Chelsea and let her know you and I both know."

"I have no clue as to what you are talking about." says Karmah.

"Baby, you don't have to lie. We will finish this conversation as he is getting out the Jacuzzi. Oh and by the way, he smelled like one of you whores." she then hangs up on Karmah.

"Your steak and potatoes with green beans on a separate plate is on the table with your peach tea light ice." She rolls her eyes after she is done telling him.

Diamond excuses herself and let the water out of the Jacuzzi. She notices long strands of blonde hair. Neither Karmah or Chelsea has long hair. She is furious but says nothing. She is going to take a step further on Sunday and see who has long, blonde hair. She cleans out the Jacuzzi, further fulfilling her normal wifely duties. But this time, she takes a shower instead of relaxing.

She runs her hot water and gets in the shower. She immediately is crying out to God because she wants to hurt him. He hurt her so deeply. She is doing all these wifely duties and does not feel appreciated. Also, how she is secretly stripping again and sleeping with some of the men to save up to leave her husband is coming to her. Instead of her praying for him and trusting God to do His will in the marriage, she takes matters into her own hands.

She cried out, "Lord make a way of escape for me. Show me your plan in my life. Expose him if you must. Please get me out of this terrible marriage, and forgive me of all my sins."

As she is praying her phone rings. It's the club where she strips.

"Hello boss. Is everything ok? You never call me."

"I was calling to let you know we must let you go. We've found out you have been sleeping with some of the men and in the contract, it stated you can be terminated."

"I understand and have a good night."

"Lord, I know that was you. I am listening Lord. Order my steps in all ways of my life."

She continues to shower letting the water run down her head and she feels a peace come over her. She starts saying, "Thank you God. Thank you for peace. Lord I need you like never before."

She gets out of the shower and gets dressed. She goes downstairs to see what her husband is doing because she noticed it was quiet. As she goes down the stairs, she calls his name twice. He doesn't answer. As she gets to the last steps, she notices he is not in the chair. she calls out his name,

"Grey? Grey?" She looks and notice his body is on the kitchen floor still and lifeless. She screams and calls 911 but he is pronounced dead on the scene.

Every Breath You Take

Breathe in, breathe out, breathe in, breathe out. What if you breathed in, breathed out, and that was it? Where would you spend eternity? Where will you be, what will you be doing, who will you be with? Will you be fussing, cussing, fighting, having sex. Every breath you take is a blessing from God. Let's not get so caught up in our own selfish, fleshly desires.

We need to come out from amongst those who are leading us to HELL also! But we also must examine ourselves of who we could have been leading to HELL! Every chance we get we need to be leading someone to Christ. God delivered us from things, but we allowed Satan to overtake us with his tactics again. Just imagine all the people we may have led astray from our Father in heaven.

As you breathe in and out, what are some things you could have done differently? Pray and ask God to show you and then write them down.

Hidden Agenda

Karmah started working a more traditional job. She began talking to Gracelynn, a lady she met in her department, about church. She could tell Gracelynn was a Christian. Karmah would ask her questions about her church. Karmah was raised in the church but wasn't really into it while she was there. She still remembers the book of Proverbs Ch. 22:6 (KJV) *Train up a child in the way he should go and when he is old, he will not depart from it.*

A talk leads to three hours in the bookstore across from the office. Memories of freedom rang in Karmah's ears and she didn't need much coaxing.

Gracelynn asked, "Do you want to be saved?"

"Yes." Karmah whispers through a single tear.

Before Karmah visited her church, they became really close friends. They would talk about all kinds of people at the church, but one particular conversation stuck out to Karmah. Hurricane.

He was portrayed as a Godly family man who had his finances in order. Karmah heard family man, and a one-woman man and thought, "Though that could be true, there is always another side to the fairy tale." After hearing about him, Karmah's conniving spirit started rising. She had to fan herself to calm her excitement.

"I'm going to turn him out, take his money, make him fall in love, and give it to him real good!"

Sunday morning came and she got up with a big stretch. With a wandering mind, she yelled out loudly for her daughter to get up and get dressed for church. Karmah found a sexy little outfit to wear to church. She showered, did all the essentials and, once dressed, grabbed all items needed for the day. As she was traveling along the highway to church, Karmah noticed the beauty of the day. She checked out the scenery, the beautiful trees, a bright sun shining. She started feeling nervous as she got closer to the church. she could feel her heart pounding.

Karmah turned into the church yard. She called Gracelynn to double check on the destination. She did not know this church or these people but she did know about Hurricane and a little about what he went through in his first marriage. She cheated on him!

"Hey friend, how are you?" Karmah asked.

"I'm good, how are you Karmah?

"Oh, I'm good. I'm a little nervous" Karmah says with a giggle.

"Karmah you're going to be fine girl." Gracelynn beams sharing the laughter with Karmah.

The pair entered the sanctuary and found a seat.

"That's Hurricane I was telling you about."

Karmah turns and looks back at the door to find Hurricane standing. The bold spirit in Karmah got her out of her chair and literally walked her up to him while he stood at the door waiting to greet God's people.

"Hello. How are you? I'm Karmah."

He introduced himself. She had readied a small slip in her hand with her number.

"Here is my number call me," Karmah said to a ready smile. "I'm serious."

She smiled her best sneaky smile as she reached out for a hug. Karmah saw the timid look on his face and she laughed on the inside knowing the work ahead. Now, Karmah grew up in the church and knew church manners- at the time, she could care less. She walked back to her seat triumphantly and whispered to Gracelynn without moving her lips,

"I gave him my number…"

Her friend laughed with a big smile on her face.

Order of service began, and Karmah at once felt out of her element. The reality that she had been out of church for years started to sink in. By now, she had come in contact with all types of spirits with the willing spirit and weak flesh battling against each other. As her head fell down and she rubbed her nails to soothe feeling out of place, her eyes moved side-to-side

"Who's watching me?" Karmah could hear the singing of praise and worship. She sat stiff as a board and noticed how her friend was worshipping God by singing and lifting her hands. Karmah was in shock because of the things they talked about, she didn't know Gracelynn was actually into the church like that. Others were worshipping Him. She was just sitting there. Though she could feel the song in her spirit, Karmah's flesh had more control.

The order of service flowed from beginning to the ending of the word. The question was asked by the Pastor of the church, "Does anyone want to join the church?

Karmah and her daughter went up and joined. It was if she could feel the people staring her up and down. Even though she joined, Karmah still felt the same way as when she first came. She was puzzled, sitting with a look of concern because she couldn't rationalize why. The congregation greeted her with love and hugs. Before church was over, Hurricane's number was on a program, hand written.

"Yes he wrote that AND gave it to me."

Karmah couldn't wait to call him. She decided that she was out to get him.

Karmah was in for something she could only ever imagine. She called him later that evening and they talked for countless hours while getting to know one another. Karmah let him know that she was in a relationship. it didn't disquiet him from wanting to chitchat with her.

"Where do you stay? I want to come over." she asked him.

"Why do you want to come over?"

Karmah announced with a bit more aggressiveness in her voice, "YOU KNOW WHY I WANT TO COME OVER, DON'T PLAY WITH ME!"

He offered all the information she needed. Her sly smile could be heard over the phone with each passing word. He was all hers.

Karmah found something to put on that was easy to access. She wanted him to know what was up as soon as he opened the door. Moments later she called him to let him know she was on the way.

He answered.

"Hello."

"I'm on my way."

"OK."

On the way, her mind began to wonder about this and that. At that moment, she had stepped into the shoes of a manipulator and a liar. She had set out to get a man who was minding his own business and trying to stay saved. She knew his flesh was fighting the same thing hers was following- LUST.

Karmah pulled into his place, walking up to the door.

She knocked.

He opened the door and she sat on his couch. He walked over and sat next to her. Karmah felt a little shy at first but his heat refocused her. She was still set to get him. Hurricane wasn't fighting the lust at all anymore.

They talked for a moment while she steadily started feeling on him. He was already in a white robe making for easy access to his dick. She continued to rub on him, as he smoothly led her into one of his bedrooms where the tables were turned on Karmah.

In a moment, Hurricane did to her what she set out to do to him. The sex he put on Karmah was nothing like the man Gracelynn told her about. To Gracelynn, he seemed like a person that you could control, and he sure didn't look like he could provide what he just put down on her.

"What did I get myself into?!?" She didn't want to leave. Breathing hard, she laid there on his chest thinking how she just had the best sex ever. Her mind was astonished as to his overall appearance and size. He started to brag on himself but there was no need. She knew there would be other times.

She even told him what she was trying to do, "Oh I know…" he responded with a smile. She then got quiet for a few seconds, eyes stretched wide and said, "How did you know?"

"I could tell."

It was like the room was spinning. He was in her head! This man knew exactly what she was trying to do and boy, was he ready. She went into the bathroom to freshen up, then she left.

She called him as she was traveling home to talk about how the sex was breathtaking…

She wanted more.

Karmah told him she would call when she got home. She was in disbelief for the whole ride home

"I'm Karmah! I'M the SOUL SNATCHER!"

She knew she had to get back over there to prove her point. The night was beautiful and a peaceful sky seemed to erase the horizon.

"Lord, please forgive me for what I just did." She even asked for forgiveness once they were done but her mind was already gone. She was confused and overwhelmed with thoughts. She had just joined the church that day and was sleeping with Hurricane the same night.

When arriving home, she did all the necessary things that needed to be done. She wanted him to sweat at least a little bit. She then called and let him know she was home. She went to bed thinking about him and her spirit was not right. That tug-of-war going on with her flesh kept her up much later than she had planned. She eventually went to sleep after thinking about their night and how it backfired on her.

As she awakened the next morning, Hurricane was the only thing on her mind. She absolutely could not resist, so she called him when she got to work. Hurricane was delighted to hear from her.

She asked, "How are you doing?"

"I'm good, how are you?"

"I miss and I want you"

"I want you too"

Karmah had the biggest grin on her face because at that moment what she set out to do was not the plan anymore. She wanted him for just one night. She didn't realize how much she wanted to be out of control. They said their goodbyes for the day because they both had to work.

She called him when she got off and told him how she felt about him. He replied, "I don't want a relationship and… you're already in a relationship as it is."

She told him she would leave her boyfriend for him. He didn't want that. That crushed her spirit, but she still felt there was a chance to get him.

Sunday comes around and she sees Hurricane in church. She goes up to him to talk to him, but he speaks as if they had never been together! "Why did he do that?!?" She could have choked him right there. In church she felt uncomfortable because they had sex and now they were in Gods house.

"He is giving praise like this is ok!" Karmah thought as she just sat there. She couldn't even look in his eyes while he sang on the praise team.

"He just might get his wish and not see me again..." Karmah intoned.

But like clockwork, Karmah was in his bed again doing all kinds of tricks, twists and turns. She was bending her back all kinds of ways to achieve whatever position he wanted. Karmah wanted to play into his desires because he fulfilled hers. She loved when he gave her hard, rough sex- when he choked her and call her names. She would make groans and moans in his ear knowing that would turn him on. They were made for each other on the sexual side.

The sex relationship progressed and that's all it was. But Karmah felt something rousing in her spirit. It was like a sex demon on the inside of her. she craved Hurricane all the time and he wanted her all the time but he felt convicted more and more afterwards. They would talk numerous times a day. They would meet anywhere to have sex: in his car, her car, his company truck, even outside at businesses. It had got to the point that this was the normal thing for them.

One night, Karmah called and was surprised to find herself talking to a voicemail.

"Hurricane always answers… Karmah don't get mad." Karmah decided a long time ago not to pop up at this house but wild thoughts ran through her mind.

She began to talk to herself, "He will not ignore me. I should punch him in his face, choke him and dig my nails in his eyes." Her anger was taking over.

"He don't know who he is playing with! I will run him over and leave the tires on his chest."

The next day Hurricane finally answers.

"WHERE WERE YOU LAST NIGHT?" Karmah said in a hostile voice.

"I went to the movies." He responds as coolly as an evening walk in the park. Hurricane can sense Karmah's blood about to boil.

"Who did you go to the movies with?" rage is filling up on the inside of her to the point that Karmah is ready to snatch him up through the phone.

"I took a new friend I met. Antonette is- "

"I thought you didn't want a relationship?" she reminded him of what he said previously while pacing through a path already worn from a restless night. She was furious about the fact he now had someone but she was not giving up at that point.

"Antonette is a nice woman. I think I'll ask her out again soon" Hurricane slowed his pace to make it clear he unbothered.

A tear begin to fall as Karmah let out the ugliest cry. Her face was all covered with tears as if someone poured water on her

"Am I having a full on breakdown?!?" Karmah thought as she mustered her parting words,

"I see."

On Sunday morning, Hurricane is sitting in church with Antonette. Karmah is a walking time bomb at this point. The look she gave him made the entire pew shudder.

"He should just leave." even Karmah's friend is upset at this point. He walks by where Karmah is sitting and speaks. Karmah gave him a look so hot he could have sworn Karmah told him to pack up and leave Florida or at least get his new girlfriend out the church. Antonette can't help but sense the wrath at this point.

"I can't stand her because she is coming between what I have with Hurricane." Karmah explains to her consoling friend. Service continues as usual.

The devil got in Karmah after church. She saw Antonette outside the church and said to Hurricane loudly, "How you gonna bring this ugly lady to the church?"

People turned and looked. Karmah grabbed her friend's hand and made her way to the back of the parking lot.

"Be the look out. I'm going to key his car." Karmah's friend was too afraid to say no. As they looked around with a faster pace walk they checked left and right trying to see if someone was looking. Karmah took her key and went back and forth down his passenger side doors. Both times, the car did not scratch.

She says to her friend with shear frustration, "What kind of paint is this?" When she was done, she felt the urge to leave. She was instantly worried she would have probably ended up in jail.

The next morning, all Karmah could think about was how Hurricane did not call her. She was so done with him.

"He could have at least told me She was coming to church. He is sexing me all these months and now he wants to bring someone openly all of a sudden? Nope!" she was not having it.

She started thinking of evil things to do to him. she could explode at any point. Hurricane didn't really know what to think or say at this point, but his silence made it even more tense.

As time went on, Karmah discovered Hurricane still had feelings for her. Before long, she ended up back in the bed again. Antonette did not do all the things Karmah did to him and every chance Karmah got with him became a part of the competition. She determined to put a working on him that he could not forget. If she could swing from a chandelier and bounce ride on top, ride him frontwards, backwards, or sideways… Whatever way she could imagine she would have done it. He brought out a side of Karmah that suddenly seemed as if it was waiting to jump out and be free. It was like a monster held in a cage had run wild as soon as the gate was cracked open. She loved how hard he would give it to her and the sound he made just made chills go through her. When they touched, it was like super glue. Even though she felt no hope at becoming his wife, she still loved him. She was now hurt and broken.

Karmah eventually changed her number to move on with her life, found another man and got married. She still was a member of the church but the feeling never really left for Hurricane. She started speaking to Antonette but deep down she felt like she was talking to a woman who had eyes on her man Hurricane.

One night after church, some women were outside talking with Antonette. She "happened" to mention her and Hurricane were getting married, so the ladies were congratulating her.

"What date did you say again?" Karmah said

"Oh, we are all set for April 17th." Antonette didn't skip a beat.

"That's my birthday…" mumbled Karmah with a look of disgust on her face. She was just out done with all the shenanigans. She never actually forgot Hurricane's number so she called.

"Hello…"

"HOW YOU GOING TO GET MARRIED ON MY BIRTHDAY?!?"

"I didn't know that was your birthday." Hurricane says in a high-pitched tone.

"How you didn't know that was my birthday?" she felt as if he never cared anything about her or her feelings. Worse, she felt he wanted to get one last dig in for no good reason. She wanted to cuss him out but she respected him enough not to. She loved him no matter what her intensions were in the beginning. She loved him.

Hurricane's marriage finally took place. Karmah just knew for a fact that the nuptials signaled the end between the two of them. Now that they were both married, they could move on. She was breathless when she saw him at church and he told her to call him. He even asked her for her new number.

"He just got married it has not even been a month."

She ended up calling they talked. It doesn't take long for Hurricane to muster the words she dreaded and longed for,

"I miss you so much."

But even at a point in their single sex game, Karmah knew he felt convicted and wanted to stop having sex with her. Now he missed her but he said, "I DO" to someone else.

Karmah eventually decided to leave that church because she had to get over him and do what was right.

Here we go again they met. They had rough sex like old times and it continued off-and-on for years. She tried to stop it by changing her number numerous times. Somehow, he located the number to her desk at work. One day, she picked up the phone,

"Karmah here. What can I do for you?"

"I'm so glad I finally can hear you again" Hurricane was pouring it on thick.

When she hung up with him, she felt a bad chest pain and she thought to herself, "What in the world is this feeling?" She the feeling with a look of fear. The feeling and then the look vanished quickly.

A couple weeks later, they talked again but all they did was talk about how good their sex together had been.

"Words can't describe how our sex life was. Honestly, I don't want nothing like it anymore. You didn't have to buy me anything, all you had to do was just give me sex like I wanted it." Karmah couldn't hold back her tongue. "I loved how you wanted me in all sorts of positions."

"You are a very flexible lady. One position that blew my mind was when you flipped your body in a way where I could see you enjoying every bit of my dick." Hurricane shuddered from the memory of her.

"I would have hung from the chandelier, jumped off and bounced right on you if you had one attached to the ceiling. I loved riding you too. I really loved to take control." Karmah's mind raced as she spoke those words

"I loved it when you got aggressive…"

After that conversation, she felt the same chest pain. At this point she said, "God I will stop. You don't have to take me out."

She gives God praise for bringing her out of the situation with Hurricane. She realized that it took much prayer and crying out to Go. It wasn't time to be cute. She was for real about wanting to get out of that situation. No matter how amazing his sex, Karmah realized it was not worth going to HELL for. Looks can be deceiving when it comes to what a man can do in the bedroom! Her scheme backfired. Tables can be turned from what you set out to do.

That Hidden Agenda/adultery/Mistress relationship ended right then after seven years off and on. God was not pleased because at that point she had a good church home and was trying to do right living by God's word.

Exodus 20:33: Thou shalt have no other gods before me.

Secret Sin

Another man, Denim, was more of the street thug type, a nonchalant warrior who didn't really let things get to him. He didn't show much emotion unless his lady did first and frequently. He was about 5'6 with a medium build and gold in his mouth. His sex was like she loved it. He left her speechless- she thought Hurricane was something but Denim was the man.

For over eight years, he wanted Karmah but she thought never in a million years would she give him a chance. Time would go by in between the years where he would stop trying to be with her. She knew all he probably wanted was sex but she never budged refusing all his advances because she knew they'd end in getting with him in the bed. She only would converse over the phone and that would only last about a couple days. For a while, Karmah felt she couldn't get into him in a casual or sexual way. The wild thing is, for the entire time they knew each other, when she would see him, joy would come over her. She wanted his attention, it was like a ray of sunshine entered with his presence.

"Yeah… I know he still wants me." she would think to herself.

She liked the looks he gave her throughout the years. Looks that occurred every time he was supposed to be visiting Karmah's cousin.

She would see him at different events but of course, he acted as if he wasn't interested. Karmah always acknowledged him with a big smile. Occasionally, he would slide messages in her inbox on social media. "Immature" she said to herself. "Does he think he is all that?"

He would message, "All your church people are on your page and I know you in the church. That doesn't mean we can't chat here."

On a particular November 22nd, Denim shoots his shot again. He knew she was still teaching God's word.

He didn't care.

He cared about the freaky side to her from previous conversations. He wanted to prove a point Karmah- that he knew how to conduct business in the bedroom. Something on the inside of him could pick up that same spirit on the inside of her.

They started going back and forth in the inbox. This time it was different for Karmah. She continued conversations with him that she would normally shut down in years past. She felt her flesh rising with things he would say. He woke up something she thought she was over, but it was just lying dormant.

He brought up how she would lie to him about them going out. He would always ask to take her out and she would say yes, but she would either come up with an excuse or he wouldn't hear from her.

Karmah tested the waters, "Hush, and give me some money... You might get more of what you want."

"I don't have any money, you have a live-in ATM machine", Denim scoffs

Karmah snapped back, "And you have live-in pussy"

Silence crowds the line...

"I won't ask you for it anymore..." Denim stops responding.

Hours go by. She couldn't take that he ended it. He had twisted the key opening the door to the old person in her. The old Karmah started rising. The attention wasn't on old Karmah anymore and she couldn't take it. She wanted him to continue to chase her. When he didn't, she had to entice him.

She went back into the inbox.

"Guess what?"

"What?"

Karmah sent nothing.

"That should get his attention." Karmah thought as a sly smile approached her lips.

He wanted her to call him, so he gave her his number again. They started texting each other for hours throughout the day and night. Karmah eventually figured it was time to make another move.

"What are you going to be doing on Thursday night?"

"I'm free. You going to be able to get out?" Denim knew she was that much closer to caving.

Karmah was married to Brock, someone he knew very well.

"Yeah. I'm gonna be ready and able." She texted as quickly as she could.

Deep down, Denim didn't believe she was going to come but on his day off, she surprised him and showed up.

As soon as she got in his car she said, "Hey." The years spent away from each other melted in that single word and they felt what they had planned was closer than ever.

"Come on, I have to hurry" Karmah begins to peel clothes as she heads toward the backseat of the car.

Denim does what he can to conceal his shock but Karmah can feel the power she commands in his surprise.

"She hasn't shown up all this time, now she's down for whatever?!?" Denim's mind races as he prepares himself for an experience.

They had rough sex right in the parking lot of the store. She let Denim in on what he'd been missing all this time.

"Yes baby I can handle you. You better come with it." she knew she had to show him what she was working with.

Karmah was like a raging bull. There was an age difference, Karmah was older, so she had to come with it.

After the bout was over, they cleaned up and she went home to Brock her husband. All she could do was think about Denim. Karmah wastes no time to text Denim letting him know how good the sex was.

They met up for the next three days straight having sex as if there were never any gaps in their communication. During sex, she would say to herself, "Yeah, I'm going to give it to you and leave..."

It was like she was out to get back at him as well. She could feel herself falling for him just that fast, but she still wanted him to chase her.

Over time, Karmah came to realization she was battling with something on the inside of her that she thought she had over-came. She would have sex with these men to get back at them but then she would always get her heart broken.

Eventually she started noticing a change in his routine a few weeks into their death sentence. It felt like playing Russian Roulette. Karmah was teaching God's word, still encouraging people, giving advice and sharing scriptures but living in sin.

"I can feel the anointing is gone. I should have never let anyone contaminate it." Karmah's inner voice never stopped crying out. She would feel convicted because she knew it was wrong. She started noticing how his text messages would come less often. It seemed like on his days off, he would text less.

By now, Karmah was loving him in a different way. She never felt love like this before but he wasn't on the same level. He'd said he loved her but was not in love with her. Karmah was surely in love with him. So when he would limit his time with her, eventually she mentioned it to him. He didn't feel the same way,

"You're seriously stressing me? Nothing has changed. We will always be together." he said the words but how could she believe them? He also had a family, but when she considered how he came at her for all those years, It would only make sense that he would try and be with her all the time.

Karmah couldn't contain her jealous thoughts but she wondered whether she craved control more than the relationship itself.

Karmah's mind was getting too deep into him. She was losing herself and like a sinking ship, she was sinking in her sorrows.

She made up all kinds of excuses to leave the house to meet up with him. She would text him in the middle of the night. He had taken over her mind as if he had a remote control guiding her life and feelings. Karmah stopped praying like she used to and even stop reading her word. She would try to see what Denim was going to do on Wednesdays. His actions would determine if she went to church that night or not.

Karmah confided in her daughter Reign about Denim. Reign couldn't help her because she was dealing with her own issues. Reign would often jokingly say to her mom, "See where I get it from?" Reign thought it was funnier than Karmah. Whenever she heard it, she remembered what ministers and even she had said about "generational curses."

Karmah would call Denim 'Soultie' when she spoke of him. She felt a living monster in her. That monster would collude with Karmah, planning the next moves to try on Denim or recalling an experience with a previous lover. In the end, all she wanted to do was satisfy Denim sexually.

She needed help but knew she couldn't tell the saints. "They are so judgmental and like to toot their noses at people instead of meeting them where they are. All that shame to end up in sin again and praying alone for the sin be removed?" Even still.

some already knew some of her past and they would probably judge her knowing in previous years she had wrecked someone marriage. Karmah cancelled the thought quickly.

She thought one day to sit herself down and do nothing in the church until she got it right. "But look how others are still doing the will of God and committing sin." Deep down she still knew she didn't want that same mentality.

Karmah has been in the church for years, how could she allow herself to let someone come in between the relationship she had with God! When you love God nothing or nobody should separate that love. Romans 8:38-39 For I am persuaded, that neither death, nor life, nor angels, or principalities, nor powers, nor things present, nor things to come, 39 Nor height, nor depth, or any other creature, shall be able to separate us from the love of God, which is in Christ Jesus our Lord.

Karmah's self-reliance led her straight into a different level. She went to Denim house and had sex with him in the same bed that he and his wife shared. She knew she wasn't the first person to have been in that bed. He was a pro at what he did and he wasn't nervous at all.

His wife would be out of town on business, or with family and friends. Karmah was nervous a little but Denim made her feel protected. One time, all she could think about was where she would hide if his wife came home, would she get shot or have to jump out the window? Karmah would scope out the room to see how it was set up and noticed red roses on the corner of their brown dresser. She started thinking he must love her. That spirit on the inside of her was taking over her body and mind and Karmah began to feel the presence of more. It felt like a camp meeting was taking place with all the different spirits. They were crafting a blueprint of what was next.

She felt a little uncomfortable but as he walked toward her with his firm bottom, she couldn't contain herself.

"Oh my, he is sexy!"

That was her first time seeing him fully naked. They had usually met in the car or some impromptu and smaller place for sex. Still, his body no doubt turned her on. The first time she made love to him in the bed, she became so dizzy she wanted to take a breather.

"That's enough Denim. Give me a minute."

He had to prove to her that he could handle her. He showed no mercy to her. Before long, she was screaming from pleasure and motioned him to stop he paused and said, "No, you can take it."

She begged him to stop knowing it was exactly what he wanted to hear.

"Please stop! I want it but I can't take it."

"You really want me to stop? I think you can take it." Denim says.

He was insatiable. He came again and again but kept going and going.

When she was able to change a position, she got up and grabbed him, "I can't take it, I'm dizzy."

"I just want to be clear... I can hang."

Karmah cleaned, got dressed and went home. As she traveled down the dark highway she seemed as if she was on the road all by herself. She said, "Lord, please forgive me! I don't know why I keep doing this."

According to the things he had told her he'd done, she knew for a fact he would do anything anywhere. He mentioned his threesomes and told her the names involved, Karmah was no-where near that level and she made it clear . At one point, she started watching pornography again. She had to talk to herself many times, "You have to stop this! God sees you." They began routinely sending nude pictures to each other. This was all a fan-tasy, she knew they could never be as one. Denim had someone, and she had someone.

She told him she wanted them to be together,

"I have it all planned out."

"Are you serious? So you got It all planned out." he said with disbelief. "I'm not happy and I think she's cheating, but we do have a child and we should work it out."

Karmah couldn't believe he wasn't down. Moving forward, Karmah didn't put anything past him. Even still, she almost made herself believe she was the only one he was sleeping with,

"Come on Karmah! You know better than that. He is just like all the other men. Break him down, make him call you first..." Karmah would coach herself aloud each morning. She would see him texting her and would ignore it. Denim would send another one saying, "Oh your phone doesn't work?" or "Get at me when you get a chance."

Karmah would smirk and giggle to herself. Still, she was hurting and wanted him to love her. She would cry silent cries and sometimes tears would fall on her pillow. She couldn't remember feeling like this for Hurricane. Denim was all she could think about

She would continually think to herself, "I should sit myself down from doing God's work. I know what I'm doing is not right."

Karmah felt contaminated. Some people she met must have been contaminated already too. Even though she prayed over herself to remove anything not like God, she still knew it had to end. Anything could have happened to her and him while they were together.

Denim and Karmah started to believe what they were doing was something like a relationship. They would tell each other they loved one another, although, most of the time she would initiate. At a point. Karmah started getting sick and tired of the same routine. They had only gone out once to the movies and even it was a little strange to her. Overall, it was a nice outing with Denim. Their relationship was really just sex, texting or phone conversation. The light flickered on in her head and a voice reminded her, "Karmah you are married, he is married, and he is not your man. You are saved and should not be doing this."

She constantly repented to God and asking for forgiveness but she still slept with him.

The relationship had lasted another eight months when she decided to really break it off. As she thought about it, it became a waste of time and disappointment to her. It caused her heartache, anger and pain.

She would often say to herself, "I think he loves me." then another time she would say, "He can't love me."

He was the type who if you ask to many questions, you were being noisy or trying to start an argument

"What a mentality to have, I'm only trying to get to know him." All these thoughts started forming back in her head.

She loved when Denim would say during sex, "You love me baby?" She would then reply, "Yes baby. you love me, you going to leave me? Tell me you not going to leave me."

His response and the way he responded reminded Karmah she was in control, and that was her plan. She had to be in control.

Karmah got too lost on her path with the Lord. She began to stalk his wife, sister-in-law and mother-in-law social media. Mostly it would be the sister-in-law's social media pages because she posted the most

One day during a routine snoop, she noticed one of his old chicks hanging out with his wife's family.

Karmah thought, "What kind of orgy they got going on at the castle?" She would stalk Denim's wife, Lovie as well. Karmah would go on Lovie's page and stare at her as if she wanted to take her out. Lovie was only spared because Karmah knew she didn't love him that much. She would do this time after time. Soon, she went even further by texting her to have double dates which they never did because of scheduling conflicts.

Karmah knew how to ask questions to find out what she wanted to know. People would never put Karmah and Denim together. Karmah mastered the art of being in the inner circle while sexing a woman's man. Karmah never stopped feeling like she had a problem she needed help to overcome.

She came to a place where when she had sex, she wanted it painful. She wanted to be choked, and other things. She lost her old desires and gained new ones. One day she blocked his number only to immediately unblock it, she was in too deep and was starting to feel overwhelming anxiety. One night, she started feeling pain when she breathed in and out. She got up because she felt she was having a shortness of breath. It started getting worse and she literally felt she was going to pass out. Karmah started to call on the name of Jesus, repenting and saying she wouldn't go back. It reminded her about when she was getting chest pains when she talked to Hurricane.

Denim had become something of a god to Karmah. She was putting him first before a lot of things. She would start texting him in the middle of church service, she couldn't focus. She literally was focused more on him than she did God I could only imagine what God was feeling that she would put Denim first over him. She knows the word says in Exodus 34:14

For thou shalt worship no other god: for the Lord, whose name is Jealous, is a jealous God.

Even at work, she couldn't focus. Sometimes she would catch herself gazing at the computer or she would keep looking at her phone to see if he had texted. It had come to a point where she felt comfortable texting him early mornings even though sometimes he couldn't talk because his wife was home. Many times, he would even come to her job and they would have sex in the car. she has gotten herself in a mess. She loved him, so if that's what he wanted, he got it. It cost her joy at times because soon came the excuses as to why he couldn't come see her. She prayed and asked God to help her get over him but she continued to do the opposite How can someone continue to do this to their mind, body and soul? She loved him and wanted him so bad. She even started giving him money and buying him things as if he was her man. Just think, that money could have been going in her household. She would even meet up with him on his lunch break for sex as an appetizer. On the way to meet to see him, she always wondered if she would make it back home or get in a car accident because she knew what she was doing was wrong. She was still getting so deep into it that it was hard for her to break from him. Again, she would pray and ask God to help her. She would even go up for prayer at church numerous times then feel so strongly in her spirit that she's not going to do it again. Soon she would end up right back on top of him, bent over or with him back on top of her. Seemed like with the warning God gave her through Hurricane, she would have learned her lesson. She needs to be sold out for God and cry out to him and give him a YES for real.

After deciding to leave Denim alone, because of experience one last night where it was hard for her to breathe and when she breathed in and out she felt a little pain, Karmah arose repenting of her sins. She promised God she wouldn't do it again. Upon feeling in her spirit to block his number, she went ahead, that and felt at ease. There was no more texting for a long while. She would find herself lying in bed wondering why she let herself get into those situations. Her mind, body and soul yearned for him. It was like he controlled her and wasn't ever in her presence.

She screamed, "Lord help. I don't' want it but my flesh wants it. Help me Lord."

Sexual Imaginations

Have you ever loved someone, or shall I say lusted for someone so bad you begin having sexual thoughts in your mind? It was as if you could feel the man inside of you? If so, speak God's word over your mind.

Karmah had a strong imagination about sex or was that really her! Each of the men she has encountered were like little missiles in her head exploding with all kinds of sexual feelings when she had her imaginations. She would sit and look off at the wall and imagine Denim making love to her. She would squeeze her vagina in and out as if he was on the inside of her. She would even begin talking to herself how she was going to give it to him the next time they got together.

Her imagination took over to the point that she could not get out of bed unless she had a sexual thought about him. It had to fulfill her flesh before getting out of bed. Literally, she could feel him inside of her. Eventually she would snap out of it. As she sat at work, she would catch herself staring off thinking about him and send him a sexual text message.

Denim wasn't the only one she would send sexual text messages to. There was this one guy she started flirting with just to be doing something. He wanted her for years and she knew it but he wasn't her type. He was too pretty for her. He had the look like he would never get dirt under his nails, but she could tell he was a freak by the messages and pictures he sent to her. She would smirk when she stood him up. She knew she could never sleep with him no matter what. She even thought about whether he would give up the cash. That still didn't persuade her. He and Denim also hung out together from time to time. He worked for Lovie's family business. He had a wife as well but didn't seem to be happy with her.

Karmah's sex drive for Denim caused her to not perform her wifely duties at home like she should. When she did, all she thought about was Denim. Karmah is not the only person in this gigantic world that has done this so no judging. She thanks God for her not losing her mind due to the sexual thoughts she allowed to take root.

Philippians 2:5-6 Let this mind be in you, which was also in Christ Jesus: Who, being in the form of God, thought it not robbery to be equal with God

Karmah felt as if she stopped hearing from God. When she got in her moods wanting to get over him, she began to focus on God and her assignments. She often wondered how those close to her couldn't always pick up when she was into the mind-battle games. If she would have not allowed him to get so much in her head like she did, she would have fulfilled more of her assignments.

Grayson even often came across her mind and he was from her early twenties. He lived the rough, club life. He was about 5'6 with gold teeth. He was clean-cut carrying a medium build topped with a sexy smile. Karmah was older than him, but he had control in certain areas. When she first saw him in his big truck with tinted windows, they made eye contact and smiled. See, she liked the rough guys that would stroke her the right way. He was her childhood friend's cousin. Karmah didn't like his sister as she was a little rude but one day, she was about to get her face punched in. Karmah kept her cool and spared her from having to go to the plastic surgeon.

Denim led her to the point of watching pornography. But what she did notice was that once she stopped being around him, that porno urge went away. To the woman who finds herself in a situation with another woman's man, what things have you been noticing you engage in when you are so into them versus growing away from them? One day she asked Denim did he jack off He answered, "Not often."

One day he was at work and she asked him to go into the bathroom stall and send her a video. He sent a video that showed him stroking his penis.

Karmah would talk dirty to Denim when they couldn't meet up for smoking hot sex. She truly wanted to talk to her friends about her struggle but didn't want to disappoint them. In situations like this, you should be able to go to someone (especially within the church) but sometimes people can be so judgmental to the point where someone could lose their life. How does God feel when we judge His people in a rude, disruptive, evil and disheartening way?

Karmah didn't have control over her mind. She was overtaken in her own fault of sin. But during it all, while Angels ascending and Descending were not agreeing with what she was doing, God's grace and mercy were covering her. There are still consequences we must sustain. If she would have sought God in all things, could things have been different?

Do you ever feel sex is always on your mind, but with someone else's spouse? Write down what you want God to do in your situation. He already knows. He just wants you to tell Him!

Law Firm Suspense

Desiree was ruthless and dominated whenever she arrived on the scene. She was tall, with a slender body, round eyes and medium mink lashes. Her full-size lips were outlined with a red lip-liner and a hooker red matte lipstick. She always walked with her head held high because she knew who she was. She was a very confident woman who knew what she wanted. She would walk like a stallion in her five-inch heels. As she walked down the hallway, she owned it. Heads turned from every direction as she walked into the boardroom at the law firm. Everyone respected her by standing, carrying her pink leather brief case, closing the door for her and sliding the chair from the table as she adjusted her leather crème color pencil skirt and leather crème-fitted blazer with diamond buttons. She sits down and uses the remote control to bring her closer to the table.

"Hello everyone, I hope you all have done your homework. What grade will you get today? The room is so silent, you can hear a pin drop. Karmah sits there looking at her like she has lost her mind.

"We are not children, we are grown men and women." Karmah stated unamused. She and Karmah have always been in competition with one another. Desiree talked over Karmah as if she never said a word. Simon who has been with the firm for over 10 years and is still bitter he is not higher rank mumbles, "Trick, we are not kids."

Desiree's body turned so fast you could see the hair fly around her face as she leapt out of the chair.

"What did you say boy?" as she stares at him with her arms folded, legs spread apart. Her muscle-toned calves defined her walk as she approached him.

"Nothing, I said nothing." says Simon.

"Get out and clock out before I make an example out of you!" Karmah can be heard throughout the floor.

Simon breaks his pencil in anger as he looks at Desiree with his blue sapphire eyes. He smirks at her to control his anger, he glints, "Be glad for the smirk, I wanted to call you a female dog."

Karmah stares at Simon from head-to-toe. She loves the scent of his cologne and his blue suit that contours his body. Desiree notices how she looks at him but says nothing. She has already heard that they have been seen out on the town dancing and drinking. She had a private detective follow them but never got the proof she was expecting to get. Simon grabs his briefcase, unlocks it and throws confidential papers in it. Those papers are part of Desiree's PowerPoint to complete a project. Simon storms out of the board room and the door slams. He grimaces revealing that was something he did not mean to do.

Desiree charges after him and says loudly, "You don't want to see the other side of me."

"You definitely already saw my other side so pause. Better yet, put your mouth on mute with the same remote you used to pull out the chair you sat in." He turns and takes three healthy steps saying, "You're still bitter from when I stopped sleeping with you. Or are you still wondering if I knocked off Karmah?"

"Hey. We okay out here?"

Josh who was one of the workers at the firm opened the door to make sure everything was ok in the hallway. The rage going on between Desiree and Simon always made him tense.

When no one responds he says, "Ok just checking."

Desiree says to Simon, "to answer your question, no I'm not bitter. I've had bigger and better, oh and longer than two minutes and one second of sex. Shall I keep going?"

He makes eye contact, walks toward her and says, "Or are you mad Karmah can out do what you thought you were trying to do? Yes, I was sleeping with her, you had my cousin follow us. Yes, my cousin! I know a lot of people in this city, so you will never outsmart me. You may have laid on your back for your position, but the table is going to turn and bite you right on those nice buns of yours."

"Karmah is my cousin. We set you up! It wasn't by coincidence she knows your soft spot" says Desiree.

Desiree laughs so loudly the receptionist came around the corner.

"Oh hi Leasure. I was just telling Simon how I was taking his money and how me and my cousin Karmah set him up. Make sure she finds all the cameras I planted in his house because you are on there a few times, I saw you in action you little stinker. Just get out of my sight, the both of you. Leasure you are no longer needed and fired." She paused with a stare of disgrace.

Leasure slinks back to her desk confused. She has five missed calls. She is the secretary, so every meeting goes through her. Her grudge-filled, evil personality came out as she deleted every message without listening to them. She demolished her desk with Windex, coffee and water.

"Oops I didn't mean to do that." Leasure boxes up only what she feels will be beneficial for her. Pulling out a flash drive as she walks over to Desiree office, she downloads everything from her computer and then pours oil in the back of it. She clips the wires and damages the power supply and surge protector. She suddenly hears loud heels coming down the hallway. She thinks it's Desiree, but as she turns to walk out, it's Desiree's boss Mr. Hershey.

"Hello Leasure. How are you?" he smiles.

"I feel distraught. Desiree just fired me."

"Come again?" Mr. Hershey says.

"I said Desiree fired me." says Leasure.

"Why would she do that? What happened?" Mr. Hershey asks.

She replies, "Long story. Do you have a minute?

Mr. Hershey needed a drink after hearing the horrible madness of Desiree. He knows Desiree has a lot of deceitful items on him as well. As he pauses and remembers taking Desiree on expensive trips and making love to her on the white sand at the beach...

"Mr. Hershey, Mr. Hershey"

"Yes Leasure, what's wrong?" he replies.

"I was calling your name. You looked stiff like your imagination went somewhere so it seems. Have you been with her?" Leasure asks with a look of surprise. He gave no response.

Karmah walks by and sees them in the office huddled and pensive as if they were scheming something.

"Well what do we have here?" Karmah walks past and gestures to Leasure, "I thought Desiree told you to leave!"

"I will go when I'm done speaking to Mr. Hershey."

Karmah calls Desiree on her phone to come to her office. "I will be there. I'm finishing up this meeting." says Karmah. "Leasure what have you done here? You have destroyed all her information. I'm calling the police this is illegal!"

"You are going to jail!" Karmah says to her. Karmah calls Desiree again, "You need to come now. Leasure has destroyed your office and Mr. Hershey is in there also."

Karmah was only mad because she was also sleeping with Mr. Hershey but that wasn't part of her and Desiree's plan. Sometimes family will betray you even while you do dirt together

Desiree finally makes her entrance. "Everybody out my office I have called the cops. I need everybody out now!

Karmah whispers to Mr. Hershey, "How is the wife doing? If my money is not deposited in the next 10 minutes, there will be no marriage."

Everything in him wants to cuss her out. The cops arrive, and they hear about the damage to Desiree office. Officer Brazen gets everyone's name and title. He then takes statements from everyone.

"Do you have any cameras set up in the office?" he asks,

Mr. Hershey says, "No. That's against the policy here I'm sure."

As Simon walks by, he hears the question from the officer and the answers from Mr. Hershey. "Desiree is the queen of cameras," says Simon.

"What are you still doing here" replies Desiree, "I told you to leave for the day."

"I was actually talking to Mrs. Hershey." he replies with a smirk on his face.

"Well you need to leave before you end up like Leasure, jobless."

Desiree must keep calm because the officer is there gathering information and she refuses to go to jail. Desiree didn't get her position with any educational background. She started as the secretary of the firm. Karmah and Desiree are cousins but battle the same demon. They both do married men; the only difference is Karmah battled with her own interpretation of men as a child. Desiree was hurt by her first love, so she doesn't care who she hurts.

Officer Brazen gathers up his information and no one was charged. Desiree had cameras, but Simon was always a step ahead of her. He just let her feel that she was on top of her game.

Desiree asks "Did you check the cameras?"

"They were blank, nothing was on them but Karmah and Mr. Hershey making out on your couch. Seems like you need to get a deadbolt for your office."

Desiree goes to Karmah to and lay her out with her words, "We are family. How could you do this to me? Just because we schemed on Simon didn't mean it was okay to sleep with every man I have!"

"Desiree I'm going to tell you everything now."

"No need to do that. I don't want to hear it. Family is supposed to stick together."

Officer Brazen says, "Is anyone here saved?"

"I am." Karmah admits.

"There are a lot of different spirits activated in this firm. Do you mind if I pray for this building?"

The officer put down a prayer that caused Karmah to repent. With snot coming out of her nose and tears flowing from her eyes, she begins to vomit and release things out of her.

In life, we should never sleep with people for a position or scheme with family and sleep with the same man/men. We must be watchful of who is amongst us. Mrs. Hershey never found out about Karmah and her husband. She was really only after his money, but after the prayer of the officer, she felt as if God was saying something to her. Things like this not only happen on television but also in this life on earth.

Generation After Generation

People are in situations where they feel being with a married man is beneficial for their well-being. But what it causes is pain not only in you, but in those who are connected to you. When you come in between a person's marriage and they have kids, it causes pain in those babies also. We must look at it in all-different views. It should never happen in the first instance but due to the mind-state, it happens. Did you know generational curses start back from decades before our parents were born? Some things we encounter are bloodline curses. We must learn to pray and submit them to God. We can't play with those spirits.

Karmah noticed different patterns even as an adult that her family had gone through and things that came in the bloodline even different types of sickness and diseases. She eventually experienced those. But mostly, she battled with being a mistress and turning into an adulteress. That curse was all through her family. Where and who did it start with? Regardless, what she had to do was end the curse with her. She battled it for most of her life, even as a cheating woman. Karmah has a testimony to help younger and older women come out and be delivered.

Karmah went to a church service years ago and the Pastor of the church gave her a scripture to read every morning. She eventually memorized it.

Psalm 91:1 He that dwelleth in the secret place of the Most High shall abide under the shadow of the Almighty.

She still stands on that verse to this day, but if she was rooted and grounded in the word, she would have understood how important the Word of God is for us to keep in our hearts. No matter what, she always believed and trusted in God. She sees how some people get mad at God when things are not in their hands. She never experienced that. She knows God made her and He knows what every aspect of her life is going to be about.

Karmah passed her demon on to her seed. Her seed even went through situations of being a mistress. It was like married and engaged men attached themselves to her as if she was a magnet. Satan, the false accuser himself, loves to attack our character. Similar to Job, I can only imagine how many times he went to God to attack her body. God sometimes gives Satan permission to touch us. Do you feel God has allowed Satan to touch you in any area of your life? Write about it and write about different generational curses you may feel are in your family. Sit down with different family members. Pray together and release them from your family.

Reign's Testimony

They say a girl's first love should be her dad, unfortunately, I didn't get so lucky. My dad wasn't around to give me the love and nourishment that I needed from him. So at 20 years old, I started looking for love in the wrong place. At 20, I was very slim and pretty with buns to stop traffic. You coulda called me 'Traffic Jam.'

I was a cashier at a local grocery store when what I thought was love found me. I was walking to the bathroom when I laid eyes on Kane. We stared at each other for what felt like a few minutes until I broke the stare down and went to handle business. When I walked out, he was there waiting and began to introduce himself to me as the manager of the overnight department. We talked for a few minutes and both went on with our duties.

As I clocked out and walked to my car, Kane was standing there waiting. From that day forward, we began to have a secret relationship. We both knew we couldn't jeopardize our jobs, so we were very low-key. We would flirt, meet up in the back room, make our separate ways outside then to the back of the building where we would talk.

One day, we had a conversation about our personal life. At that moment, I found out he was married and had a two-year-old child. I should've stopped there with only a couple of months in and my dignity intact. But the exact attention I was missing, he was giving to me. I decided to continue to enjoy the ride.

At exactly one year, I quit my job there and went on to work for another employer. Still, Kane and I decided to pursue each other. One night, I invited him over and he came on his meal break. We had our normal conversation that included lots of jokes and laughs, but on this particular night, we exchanged laughs for moans! That's right, we had our first kiss and one thing led to another. We ended up having sex in the front seat of his car.

There were so many things going through my head, but they weren't damaging enough for me to stop. When we were finished we just stared at each other for about five minutes. I broke the silence by telling him to get back to work and call me later.

At this point, we called ourselves being in a "relationship." After about three months, I got a phone call from his wife telling me that she knew everything. She immediately began degrading my character as a woman. Now me being the person I am, I don't take no MESS! I told her that I didn't owe her anything- her husband did- and that she better not ever call my phone again. At this point Kane tried to end the relationship. I was so angry inside because once again, the love I was missing was taken from me.

I began to call the wife's phone and threaten her. I left her nasty voicemail and text messages. She threatened to call the police so I stopped it all together. It had been a few weeks since I talked to Kane.

I was at the movies one day and I heard a voice say, "Reign." I turned around and I'm faced with Kane's wife. The look on her face would've sent chills through your body. We had a conversation as if I had never almost torn her family apart.

As time went on, Kane and my relationship began to fade. He still called me from time-to-time after the incident with his wife, but eventually contact stopped all together. I always vowed to NEVER look for love in all the wrong places again, but like they always say, "NEVER SAY NEVER!"

Silent Killer

Many of us go through life with different secrets; secrets that will even kill us. What secrets are you holding that you just can't hold in anymore? God is listening and waiting to hear your voice. God loves us so much, he will cover us and remove us from situations, people and places that are not good for us. We pray and ask God to remove us from situations. When he does, we jump right back in the bed again. What will it take for us to really stop this madness? It not only hurts us, but it hurts all that are involved even down to kids. Kids are seeing their families destroyed and not understanding why. Secrets start when you hide, tell lies and cover up your mess.

Silence can cause health issues, headaches and pillows wet from our tears. Karmah had many silent cries when she was either at work, in her car or at home with her family. When she couldn't hold it in and her eyes would be red, she would say her allergies were bothering her. She wanted Denim so bad she would scream on the inside, "Why Lord why?" Her turmoil would cause hurt after hurt and she couldn't come to grips as to why. Headaches would form. She would take deep breaths in and out. There would be days she would sit in her bed and look at the dark beige walls trimmed in white. She would hear the fan blowing and close her eyes for peace. She often would listen to ocean music on her sleepless nights. She wondered how we as women could go through this. Karmah must remember she got herself in this situation because she was out for revenge and to cheat first.

There is a special word in the book of Romans (8:28)

And we know that all things work together for good to them that love God, to them who are the called according to his purpose.

Karmah had a purpose in life to fulfill. She did the work of God even in her mess and trial. She often would feel guilty for what she was doing to the point she wanted to stop ministering. Yes, she repented but she kept doing it.

Asking herself over and over, "Does he love me?" wasn't enough for her. She needed to hear it. She felt sometimes she was in a world all by herself. But she wasn't.

All around this world there are people battling with the same demon and wanting out. Some people don't want out because of money, cars and jewelry or because they have been hurt so many times, they'd rather have someone else's man so they don't have to commit to a relationship. But when death comes knocking, then what? What if you are in the middle of sex and God shows you His face? We must remember God sees all and knows all. He made us. He knows our every thought before we even think.

Why did Karmah have to go through all she went through? As she told part of her testimony at church, she found out what others went through also and wanted to come out.

Some women are so damaged they don't even care about the other woman's feelings. Men aren't free from their share of the sin either. Brokenness and mistrust can cause spirals of damage that leave havoc and confusion in their wake...

Mixed Emotions

Watching love scenes triggers some emotions on the inside of what love really is. She would imagine if she could have a love like she saw on the television. She loves love stories. Just seeing a man give his all to a woman... Remember, she grew up seeing men cheating, so to see this sent her in an emotional state of mind drifting off thinking what if that was her. She felt her heart flutter, with a silent moan. It was as if she wanted to cry. Lord she thought why she had to go through all of this. Did Karmah know what true love really was? I think she was a woman who always knew what she wanted but wanted to have the ball in her hand. But life and relationships aren't about being one-sided. It's about knowing the person, loving, trusting, respecting, communicating and being there through the good and bad times. She sees different relationships and sometimes wishes she had it that amazing. But she knows we all go through different things in life and often people put up this persona portraying that everything is amazing. Sometimes behind closed doors could be cussing, fussing, punching, throwing, stabbing, arguing and so much more.

We must learn to love for real. First, love ourselves and know what we stand for. Love how God made you. We need to forgive ourselves for things we have done and are not happy with. Then, forgive those who we have allowed to do us wrong. Some heartaches were self-inflicted due to the things we wanted and how we wanted it. Often, she gets confused when she sees and hears people talk about others being with other people's men, because those same people would say, "Never judge. We never know what people go through to cause them to do the things they do." So, she had different emotions about different areas.

This Can't Be Happening Again!

Secret scars were getting the best of Karmah but didn't take her out. She conquered whatever came her way. She often went to church, different conferences or workshops trying to break free of what she was battling. But when she got tired of being sick and tired, she started seeing God's promises moving rapidly for her. She was even able to focus on her purpose and move forward in helping others.

She began to flourish because she put pressure on her purpose and what she wanted began to manifest. She learned to not worry about what others felt about her. She knew God had a plan for her life. When it was all said and done, she had to become accountable for her action. She often wondered why people with judgmental opinions about the mistakes of others never felt they should have been praying and lifting the next sister up.

We all must go before God. We will be judged for talking about one another and bringing others down instead of praying for them. Even now, there is someone waiting to hear our story and encouragement to bring them out.

We must fast and pray no matter how hard it gets. If your stomach start talking, talk back to it! Let it know you need a breakthrough. It's time out for playing. No one wants to die leaving their purpose unfulfilled. If you must cry out with snot on your face, cry out and let it flow.

When Karmah was praising God thanking him for bringing her out, she was shouting like her life had been made brand new and nothing could cause her to turn back. Imagine Karmah running around shouting like she was free and delivered from all her mess. She was prophesying to herself and making affirmations.

My Lord! A day later, she would find herself right back in the bed of Denim. Furious and not believing it could happen again, she would cry out to God overly distraught about her actions. This man had control over her. She was numb and finding herself wanting to pull her hair out. She really wanted to be free of him no matter how he made her feel.

Reflecting on her life as a cheater, fornicator, mistress and adulterous, she felt like a habitual criminal. Karmah felt unworthy because she knew she let God down again. This was the time she needed to really put an expiration date on the end of her sinful ways. Karmah needed to decide what would go in the dash between her birthdate and death date on her tombstone. She would soon find herself at the altar getting prayer when a word given to her would made her really know God was not playing. She went to another church service and screamed for God to remove every residue. Though she still thought about Denim from time-to-time, she still felt she would never sleep with him again. She still often thought about him, but even that ceased. Months passed, and she got a text message from Denim. Her response was something she should not have done.

Oops I Did It AGAIN

The Finale of a Mistress

Karmah's last encounter as a mistress was with Denim. Karmah was in her upstairs room when she heard a knock. A puzzled look fell upon her face because she knew hardly anyone just popped up at her house. She stretched her thick body and jumped up with only her red lace thong on showing off her plump, round booty. She slinked up to the front door as quietly as she could. Once she reached to the door, she stood on her tippy toes because she was too short not to. She looked out the peep hole. Her face looked as if she saw a ghost.

She blurted out to herself, "This fool has lost his mind."

The feeling through her body almost made her pass out. She took in deep breaths trying to get her heart rate under control. Her phone rang while she was at the door.

"Open this door." Denim said as he began to bam on the door. Karmah said, "Leave my house before I call your wife."

Denim couldn't care less. Karmah realized this and gave in.

She opened the door to his sexy body standing there in front of her.

"What's your problem? What's been going on?" Denim grunted as he moved closer to her with his strong, built body barely contained by stone washed jeans. Karmah felt chills going through her as he walked towards her. Her heart was beating too fast. As she took deep breaths in and out, he could see her chest heaving up and down. Her eyes watered as she battled with her flesh. He was standing right there and she wanted to pass the test but as his hand slid down to her vagina, her eyes rolled up and down. The intense heat she felt was intoxicating. Sensing her buckling, he did it again as his tongue moved up and down her cheek. He remembered her exact spots. She grabbed him and pulled him into the house. Unzipping his pants, he pushed first her lower ribs, then her hips to the floor. He divided her legs and began to stroke her vagina with his tongue.

She released a deep moan but in her mind, she pondered, "How could I allow this to happen?"

She steadily began rocking her body as he licked her all over. She mustered the resolve to take control as she hopped up and pulled his pants down.

It happened so fast that he exhorted, "Dang baby, you strong!"

Undeterred, she pulled him closer and stroked his hardening shaft up and down. Looking into his eyes, Karmah said to herself, "Make him hurt like he hurt you."

She gave him a grin as she pulled him inside her as if to say, "Yes baby, I want you."

"What was that?" Karmah said with fear in her voice. She feared her husband Brock had to be waiting just around the corner. Denim couldn't look because Karmah obscured his view. He really didn't care either way. He was squeezing her so tight, she couldn't move.

Denim turned her and bent her over. He inserted into her hard with no mercy. She tried to hold back screams. It almost felt as if someone punched her in the face. Denim knew she wanted nothing else to do with him so he wanted to punish her vagina. He knew that's how Karmah loved sex; rough, hard and unyielding. As she screamed he said, "You going to leave me baby?

She didn't say anything so he continued his work and again said, "You going to leave me baby?"

"No baby." Right then, Karmah knew should have said, "YES."

"Choke me baby. Do it hard, let me ride it." her drive for control kicked in just like Denim knew it would.

"She just has to control the man no matter what. But not today..." Denim refused her command.

He pulled her hands toward him as she was bent over. He gave it to her just how he knew she wanted it. He put his hand around her neck and applied just enough pressure. Soon he was releasing in her. As he finished, he passed out on the floor. Karmah screamed for Denim.

When she recovered, she stepped over him and peeked outside. Karmah saw her Brock just outside talking to the neighbor across the street. Panic flooded her face as Karmah writhed in confusion. She had no clue what to do. She paced from Denim to the door.

Suddenly, a familiar phone rang. It was Denim's. Karmah checked his phone as the ringing continued.

"Why is Amayzin calling Denim?"

Karmah didn't answer. She pressed ignore, then immediately looked through his text messages. They had been texting numerous times.

She kicked him hard, "Get up bastard, get up!"

When Denim didn't move, she checked his breathing. She didn't feel any air, so she called 911.

The ambulance was there in less than 3 minutes. She explained to them what happened,

"We were having sex and when he was done, he passed out. I thought he was resting but noticed that he was not breathing right."

Meanwhile, her husband who couldn't contain his excitement, had to share his plans with the neighbor.

"I got her the car she is always talking about. She's gonna love it!"

Brock took a roundabout way into the back alley to surprise her with her new car. He just missed the paramedics making their way toward the front. "I hope the neighbors are okay and no one is blocking my driveway!" Brock thinks to himself.

Karmah and paramedics came out of the house and she immediately noticed Brock wasn't in the front yard. Karmah breathed a sign of relief believing herself to have dodged a serious bullet.

Brock realized the paramedics would block his path as he was pulling the new car around. He parked and exited puzzled and growing with the fear of his wife being in danger.

"What the hell is going on?" Brock attempted to shout over the bustle of the growing crowd.

He then sees his friend on the stretcher. Brock turns pale as he sees bystanders pointing and then turning their heads away from him to avoid his rising shame. Brock's heart sank as he began to put the scene together in his mind.

As Karmah approached and immediately tried to explain, Brock erupted.

"I already heard you had been sneaking and seeing him, I just didn't want to believe it. I was going to get an investigator to follow you but I didn't see the need to."

"I stopped seeing him Brock. He just popped up over here. I stopped seeing him months ago… He stopped breathing" she says as they looked at one another.

Rage-filled tears fell from his face.

"I don't care if he dies."

Her heart's beating was uncontrollable. As they worked on Denim, a paramedic yelled out, "His phone is ringing. It says wife."

He answered and explained to her to meet them at the hospital.

Karmah and her husband stood there going back and forth. She continued to tell him she ended it months ago. Brock had the look as if he lost everything in life as it all settles in. He gets in his car and speeds off.

Karmah hears the squeal of the tires as the car bends one corner. The revving engine begins to fade a bit but after a prolonged screech, Karmah hears a loud crash. She runs around her street corner in what seems like a second to see the brand-new car wrapped around a utility pole. Bystanders follow and help to pull him out the car. Brock looks at Karmah with a hurt and emptiness in his eyes.

She feels as if the world fell on top of her. Karmah falls to the ground screaming with a scream that sends chills through even her husband's body.

"LORD NO, NO, NO LORD I'M A MESS WHAT NOW!"

A tear runs down Brock face as he squeezes her hand and gasps for air. She begins to pray for her husband to a point where he begins to call on Jesus himself.

Brock says "Lord if I would have followed the walk you had prepared for me, would it have been different? Forgive me Lord. I surrender. I will do your will."

More paramedics arrive and ask everyone to step back so they can check him out. They check his heart, pulse, temperature and ask assessment questions to make sure he hasn't lost any memory. Moments later a paramedic pulls Karmah to the side and asks, "Are you the wife?"

"Yes, I am." She says with a stern voice.

"And your name?"

"Karmah" she said confused as to the nature of the questions.

"Ma'am, that's not the name he gave me..." his voice remained calm. "Oh, what name did he give you?" Karmah had no desire to defend her marriage to a stranger no matter how shaky her foundation actually was.

"Ma'am calm down. In situations like this, a person may not realize what they were asked."

"Oh no tell me what name he said." she points her finger in his face. He backs up a couple steps, "Ma'am, we must go. They have him prepped to take him to the ER." The paramedic walks off.

Karmah follows them, but is sure to call to check in on Denim. She has inside connections at the hospital and she finds out he is in emergency surgery. Her head begins to spin, her heart palpitates. She pulls over because it feels as if she going to pass out.

Meanwhile, the ambulance is on the way to the hospital with Brock. Cars are blowing because the tail end of her cobalt blue jeep is in half of the other lane. She started calling on the name of Jesus for his grace. She prays for healing for Denim and Brock. Her head is still spinning as if she is going to pass out. An officer pulls up and asks,

"Ma'am, is everything alright?

"Yes. I'm just getting myself together. My husband was in a car accident."

"Ride behind me. I will get you there without stopping."

They pull off and, in less than five minutes, she arrives at Greater Grace hospital leaving her car at the valet. She runs in the hospital. As she approaches the doors, she sees Denim's wife and another chick she knows he used to mess with before her. They still hang out and drink shots together.

"I guess I always wondered did his wife know. Then again, with all the stuff he told me she like to do, she probably knows." Karmah walks passed them as if she doesn't see them. She feels a sudden tap on her shoulder. She turns around and it's Denim's wife.

Karmah speaks, "Hi how are you? I heard Denim was here. I-"

"You didn't hear it tramp, he was at your house. I got information from the paperwork about what happened. It also said he had a minor heart attack!"

Karmah did her best to contain her shock. The other chick he was messing with was named Creep, at least that is what the streets called her. Creep started looking Karmah up and down

"I know you're not looking me up and down with disgust. You've been with Denim for years and you're standing here with his wife?"

Denim's wife turned around looking like fire came from her face. Creep immediately starts to walk out of the hospital with the wife flying behind her.

"Yes she's nasty too!" says Karmah.

"Ma'am, Ma'am you can come on back." the receptionist motions to Karmah. Karmah holds up a finger as she is trying to see what's about to happen.

"Attack on guard, attack on guard!" an off-duty EKG tech yells out. Creep was trying to pull the guard out of the guard booth for protection.

"Satan loose me!" the guard announces and Creep immediately backs off. She runs toward the valet parking lot. Lovie jumps out between the cars where she was hiding while watching Creep try to pull the guard out of the booth.

"How you be all in my face and have been with my husband?"

"That was many years ago. why would I mention that?" Creep cries. Lovie says, "Mention it because it shows honesty for the next chick. I can't trust you, I thought you were different from other females, that's why I don't get close to females. Yall laughing, giggling and touching but don't worry. I'm not going to drag you across this pavement parking lot and mess up your pretty brown skin with these rocks cutting your face, having blood streaming down. I won't kick you in the face with my wedge heel."

How can people allow unnecessary life issues to distract them while a more serious situation has occurred with a loved one.

Karmah arrives in her husband's room after all the chaos. He's hooked up to all the machines. He opens his eyes when he hears her call his name. Brock holds out his hand the best he could, so she can come closer.

"Who did you tell them your wife was?" says Karmah indignantly.

He points to the tube in his nose, "Oh you can use your mouth, there's nothing in it. Your nose doesn't need to talk." Karmah says as her hostility grows.

"Ma'am, you have to lower your voice. The patient doesn't need to get upset, thank you." The nurse says as she walks out the room.

"You better be glad you can't get up." Karmah's eyes lower to meet Brock's.

He closes his eyes then opens one of them half way to see if she is still looking at him.

Brock whispers, "I told them you are my wife."

She just looks at him without saying a word.

"Go check on Denim, that's where your heart is. If you allow another man who was my friend, to come in our home, we can't work that out anyway." Brock doesn't know what hurt more, the revelation or the crash.

"I don't want him, but I'll be right back."

Brock's heart sinks further. He doesn't believe her. He can't.

Karmah's phone rings.

"Yes. What do you want?"

"Hey friend, how are you? I heard you had the block hot at your house today! Where you at trick?"

"If it isn't my trifling friend." Karmah thinks. She looked at the phone then looked around thinking her friend was somewhere near enough to see her.

"Hello Karmah... You there?" Amayzin asks.

"I'm here, I just wasn't sure who the hell you calling a trick."

"What is wrong with you today?

"Oh where should I start? Oh wait, I want to hear what all you heard Ms. Amayzin."

"Karmah girl, they say you had another man in your house when Brock wasn't home. Then I heard you had Denim in the house, the ambulance came and that Brock was in a bad accident."

"Well friend, Denim showed up unexpectedly."

"What? Are you serious?!?" Amayzin is in shock.

"Yeah. We was having our usual rough sex like old times and when he finished, he passed out." Karmah started to relive the tryst.

"Dang girl, you put it on him." Amayzin bellowed proudly.

"Yes hunny! I remembered that all of a sudden, his phone rang. It was probably one of his nasty women. I didn't' answer because at that time I was in a bad situation." Karmah waited a second to drop the hammer.

"Huh…" Amayzin responded without thinking.

"But Amayzin girl, it seemed that if he was laying pipe to you too, he would have had your number under a different name! Yeah you was calling when we finished up, imagine that." Karmah's jealousy began to shine through

"Who name??" Amayzin squeals.

"Your name tramp… Your name came up don't play dumb!"

"Why would he have my name saved in his phone? We don't call each other." Amayzin is obviously lost for words.

"You are such a big liar! I saw the text messages and my name was mentioned." says Karmah.

"I promise you it wasn't me. I would never do you like that." Amayzin responds with a sincere voice.

"We will get to the bottom of it" say's Karmah "and I don't even want him. I don't know why I allowed myself to get caught up in the same heartache." Karmah slams the phone in Amayzin's ear and continues to go about her way.

"I heard she was the cause of the two men being here…" nurse Green says sitting at the nurse station. "She should be ashamed of herself."

"Who are you talking about?" says a startled nurse Red.

"The lady right there with the blue stretch jeans and wife beater."

"Oh my God!" nurse red can't process what she's heard, "I know her! she is a powerful woman of God."

"Well she allowed the enemy to use her today." nurse Green snips.

Karmah heard everything but didn't have the strength to respond to them.

"...I'm going to pray for this trial in her life because we all fall, we just need some praying women that will intercede for her and all the women going through a test and trial in their lives." nurse Red says with new determination.

"Well I'm not where you at I guess, so pray for me also." nurse Green doesn't skip a beat.

"AMEN." says nurse red.

Karmah goes back into Brock's room and pulls out the chair bed. She walks up to nurse Green, the one she heard talking the most about her. "Hello. How are you doing? Can I please have a warm blanket." Karmah's pride is broken.

"Yes ma'am, just one moment."

As she goes to get the blanket, Karmah asks nurse Red, "How are you doing? How is your day going?"

"Going great! I will not complain because God is so good to allow me to wake up and get it right! I may have messed up, but this day allows me to make things right again."

Nurse Green stood back until they finished talking.

"Oh thank you Jesus." says Karmah. "I needed to hear that. I messed up for many years and today, it came down on me like a bulldozer. It felt like every weight was thrown at me and hit me one-by-one."

"Can I pray for you?" nurse red asked with an outstretched hand.

"Yes, yes, yes. Please" says Karmah.

She put a prayer on Karmah who fully let go weeping unto God. She fell to her knees squeezing nurse red's hand. Nurse green was crying as well. They all cried out to God together. They prayed for what seemed like hours. They spoke life over Karmah and ended with a group hug. Karmah was so thankful. It gave her the hope to keep pushing through what she was facing.

Karmah went back and laid in Brock's room Within a few moments, she fell asleep. She is awakened by a knock on the door. Karmah sees Denim's wife on the other side crying.

"How can I help you?" says Karmah with a blank stare.

CONCLUSION-

LIFE OR DEATH

Karmah lived a very dangerous life. Different topics show things that happen in real life. Some people are silently living a life of Hell and it is not only women but men as well. In life, we need to seek God's face like never before. Psalm 91 is a very familiar passage to so many believers. You may be fighting a battle on the inside that you need help to win. Karmah wanted help but the demon she battled with continued to win many times. Seek help and don't be ashamed. We all battle with something, some battle harder things in life the bible says in Luke 22:32, "But I have prayed for thee, that they faith fail not; and when thou art converted, strengthen they brethren."

Karmah was attractive, she had the sex appeal like fire. She always felt she was untouchable as if no hurt, harm or danger could touch her. She felt that way since she was a child. God sometimes reminded her of a thirteen-year-old Karmah sitting in the church she grew up in. She was sitting on the right side of the church on the third row from the back. She remembers high school; dating a guy when one her friends slept with him behind her back, ended up marrying him and later ended that marriage in divorce. Her life always played on replay. She never forgot the things people said or did to her. And once the tables turned, Karmah was vicious and uncontrollable in many ways. Her mind constantly thought and wondered.

It is the 'Battlefield of the Mind' as I would call it. She has many decisions to choose from. Her life is a never-ending story. She has many chapters of story to speak on, and no one will ever figure her out regardless of how hard they tried.

She had a spirit in her that wanted to sex a person wherever. It didn't matter to her as long as she was in control. Making love was never her thing. She was used to roughness so that slow motion would only leave her looking at the ceiling saying to herself, "I wish he would hurry up and finish." She was good for faking an orgasm…

She would often tell God He had to deliver her because she couldn't do it on her own. She broke down and told God, "I love it, I want it."

God already knows he just wants to hear our voice and honesty. He is an all-knowing God. She knew if she really wanted to be delivered, she had to obey God at any cost. She had to get deliverance; how could Karmah continue to lay hands on people and transfer those spirits to others (and yes, spirits are transfer-rable)?

God is waiting on us. He has so much in store for us. Will you choose eternal life in Heaven or burn forever in Hell? Has any-one caused you so much trauma that you just don't know where to turn? Cast all your cares upon the Lord, He Is waiting on you. It is not easy all the time because we want to satisfy our flesh. Imagine how Jesus feels when we continue to sin while he died for our sins. Yet we keep picking up the sins he delivered us from.

Warning comes before destruction. Ezekiel 33:5 says, "He heard the sound of the trumpet and took not warning; his blood shall be upon him. But he that taketh warning shall deliver his soul."

Why do we wait for sickness and death to scare us into doing right? We should not wait to be in the casket to stop. We want to get it right before the Rapture comes.

What will you be doing when the Rapture comes? Don't be bent over in some other woman's bed with her husband… Don't get caught. Repent and do it right now.

Don't beat yourself up for what you have done. Forgive your-self because when you repented, you were forgiven. Don't feel you are worthless; many people may scandalize your name, but they have to remember it could be them next. Know your worth and know who you are in Christ. You may even feel no one wants to be around you. Remember God will make your enemies your footstool.

With Karmah, the more she went back, the worse it was for her to get over it. God gave her a way of escape but she kept turning her back on Him. How many times will God have to deliver you? At one point, she may as well have picked out her casket and clothes after laying the program out because she was making her bed in Hell. She had allowed evil to consume her mind. She developed an attitude and would even hit men if she had to. She had a full-blown abusive side. She was not going to be the one to get hit on anymore. Karmah still lives but with a new lease on life.

Psalm 119:105 Thy word is a lamp unto my feet, and a light unto my path.

One day as Karmah was allowing God to order her steps. She was reminded of men she had been with that she forgotten all about. She began to pray them out of her soul, so nothing would come up later concerning them. Karmah always repented, she forgave herself and those who hurt her. She asked God to forgive her for those she misused.

Get deliverance. Go back to the age that things started happening to you. Karmah released things by talking about her past with different people close to her or in a general conversation.

She would find comfort in their answers. She even had friends in ministry that had been where she was.

Karmah got deliverance more than once but what made her be serious about it was the chest pains, shortness of deaths and all the deaths she would hear about. Imagine getting chest pains for something not worth dying for, like a wet vagina and more lies and sweet nothings. When you know your worth and the God you serve, you will walk in your purpose with confidence and boldness. Karmah knew who she was. she loved God for real she didn't want to die a tragic death due to not seeing and hearing all the warning signs.

She got prayer after prayer, purge after purge, fast and fast. When she fasted, she felt the presence of God like never before. She read different scriptures that would come in her spirit. She then start feeling she was more than a conqueror through Christ Jesus. When fasting people may feel you are being funny because you are spending less time with them and on the phone. Sometimes you may have to get someone you really and truly trust to help fast and pray with you.

Everyone fasts differently but you should always seek God's face. Save you from you. Your stomach may growl, talk and scream for food; you know what you need and what you need deliverance from. Lay hands on your stomach and let it know it has to line up with what you are fasting for. You may have to lay out on the floor and cry louder. Play some worship music and read that word to get it on the inside of you. Get some water and trust God is going to see you through. Everyone fasts differently so please be led by the Holy Spirit when you fast. Get your break-through no matter who walks out of your life. Your life depends on it. You have to call out those generational curses from as far back as the parents of your parents' parents.

Karmah started feeling lighter because she had been carrying unnecessary spirits that didn't belong to her at all. On one Sunday morning, she went up for prayer for one thing, but a Pastor began to pray for what God showed him and what she had pre-viously wanted to confess about. He told her don't go back. A week later at another service, as the woman began to pray, she laid hands on Karmah and started removing the residue. Karmah was serious about being delivered. She screamed, shouted, jumped with everything in her telling as God did the work to take the trauma off of her. She needed freedom.

Imagine carrying a backpack all your life full of brings and stones with different spirits talking and manifesting. She screamed for generations to come. She didn't care if snot ran down her lips, shin or on the floor. She refused to lie in a casket to end her affairs but she allowed true deliverance and God's warning to set her free.

She had to realize she was killing people and they were killing her. She loved Denim and it was very hard to let go, but she knew her reward in heaven was much greater than amazing sex and wet panties.

Get delivered and save someone else. When you tell your testimony, but honest and transparent. Let them know if you loved his sex and you didn't want to give it up. Earn that trust so you can be a mentor or a life coach. Ignore negativity and smile. God is going to prepare a table for you in the presence of your enemies (Psalm 23:5). When people scandalize your name, they have to remember they have a name also. Their skeletons may fall out right in front of their family and friends and their lack of grace can become reflected back to them.

Karmah caused a lot of stressful things due to her own flesh. Her flesh shaped a lot of her trials and she couldn't blame anyone but herself. She also had to catch herself at times for judging others who were going through the same thing she had come out of but at different points, she found herself back in it. We have to be careful what we say about God's children.

Questions to think about:

Why should you continue to sleep with another woman's man? He is probably not going to leave her. If he does, what do you think he will do to you?

Why do you think he will leave his wife?

Why do you feel comfortable in the other woman's house while she not home?

What if Jesus comes while you are in their home?

What if the woman comes home to find you and her man in a sexual position and she killed you both? Have you given this an honest thought?

Why are you so bitter and want to date only married men?

How do you feel being the Mistress to your Pastor who has his wife sitting with him on Sunday morning? He then talks about women/men who sleep with married men, fornicate and commit adultery.

Is there a specific reason why don't you want to be delivered?

Which season or seasons did you allow someone to make you miss your overflow of joy and abundance? Like Karmah, some have been chained for many days, months, years and decades. If you still want to have that Mistress title and you feel you are untouchable, God will end it sooner than you think. Karmah didn't want God to put his hands on it because He can cause either her, him, or both to die in their mess. Thank God that He didn't allow her to die in her mess.

When Denim gave her the business, she lost focus on her ministry which she wanted to stop doing. He had her mind so gone and it was not just the sex, she realized she loved his laugh and smile.

Karmah even prayed that all those acrobatic positions during sex wouldn't hinder her in years to come. Pray for every area of your body to be healed and pray that it was never contaminated.

Ladies, let's walk in freedom and respect our bodies so we can be free to help little girls. As they are coming up in a world that has sex and lust, let us save the girls and women.

God won't send your husband when you are choosing to remain with someone else's husband. Don't allow the husband God has for you to die waiting. Get your flesh right and submit your body to God.

Don't be like Karmah who kept looking back into her past and trying to get revenge. Move forward in your purpose; don't take your purpose to the grave unfinished. Go to the grave empty. Leave your fullest legacies on the Earth fulfilling all the things God has assigned you to do. We all have done things we are not proud of. Let's not judge one another as it brings us down. Remember, while we never know why people do the things they do or what they have been through, we should pray more for one another.

Prayer

Abba father, we come submitting our whole bodies to you- bodies that you created. You know us better than we know ourselves. You designed and created us in your image. Help us to live up to that image and your design for our lives. We are fighting battles that we don't want any more. Help us, O God, with your everlasting power and love. Saturate us with Your Holy Ghost power. Arrest us for your glory. Heal us of all our infirmities. Save us and set us free from our lesser selves. God, you are our all and all. Without you we are nothing. Thank you for saving us from dangers seen and unseen. You are powerful and mighty in all ways. In truth, create in us a clean heart and renew the right spirit within us. Hide us in the shadows of your wings Lord. We will not lean on our understanding, but in all ways we look to You to direct our paths. Hide us from that which is trying to overtake us. We repent of all things knowing and unknowing.

These things we pray in Jesus' name,

Amen.

Testimonials

What does Sabrina mean to me? Sabrina is a kind and fully developed woman who knows her strength. Her wisdom is unmatched, and she will always find the kindness in others when they can't see it in themselves. She inspires me to fall on my faith and trust my path. I'm glad that I am able to call her a friend and I've never doubted her intentions.

Love you, mama still got it.

-Antonette, BA

Greetings to all in the name of Yeshua!

It is indeed a blessing to share with you about this wonderful woman of God, Evangelist Sabrina Haynes! I met Evangelist Sabrina Haynes through divine connections. We were at a church service and God connected our spirits very soon after. As I began to know her, I found her to be a fun-loving and caring person. She carries a personality that draws the deepness of caring from your heart.

Knowing her over the years, I found her to truly love God and His people. In sharing our lives as friends, I have found her to be a friend indeed. There's nothing she wouldn't do for you. She loves God with all her heart and carries the same love for people.

As a friend, she has shown forth much love and caring for many years and I've known her to always be the same, never selling out or changing. I bless the Lord for connecting us. I believe that has God placed us in each other lives because we have produced from His seed of real love, we both carry His seed of righteousness toward each other to maintain what began in us many years ago; a real friendship.

CONGRATULATIONS! Evangelist Sabrina in the writing of this book, I am confident that it will bring deliverance to many. May God bless and keep you, may He make His face to shine upon you and give you peace.   -Minister Freddie Evans

Sabrina,

One of the most amazing people I have met in my lifetime. She's motivational, kind-hearted, goal-oriented, and most of all loves Jesus Christ. I always like to tease Sabrina because she's such a busy woman, but one thing I do know is she'll cross oceans for her family and close friends. I've witnessed Sabrina minister God's word to people at work, in schools, and even women in the jail. I've only known her for a short period of time, but it definitely feels like years. So happy to have someone like Sabrina in my life.

-Brenesha S. Henderson, MA

To an amazing Woman of God and Friend,

It gives me great honor to celebrate you for your accomplishment on writing your first book. I am so very proud of you. I can remember when we first met at church, you were so shy and timid. You sat in the back and didn't say anything, unless it concerned little Princeton, but look at you now. You have grown from being a babe in Christ to being a spiritual giant in this region. You did not allow your past to dictate your future. Instead you are using your past to empower and help others. because if God be for you, then who can be against you? Now instead of sitting in the back of the church you are in the pulpit speaking, preaching, and declaring the word of the Lord with boldness and power. You are an Evangelist, the next best-selling author, and my friend. My prayer is that God will continue to give you wisdom, favor, and blessings. Keep allowing your light to shine so that others will see what I see; a phenomenal woman.

I love you friend,

-Imprice Johnson

To my dear friend,

I've known her for many years. The growth that has taken place in Sabrina I must say is phenomenal. Watching her grow spiritually is pleasing to my heart. Sabrina I'm beyond proud of you. You did it! You answered the call. Now God has blessed you over and above. Your life speaks of it all.

Love,

Berta

I've known Sabrina for 40 years. She has overcome many obstacles on her journey. She was a teenage mother. She was caught up in a whirlwind for many years but one day, something happened. She found her Lord and Savior and I have personally seen the hand of God move on her behalf. She went from being a Master Manipulator and sex addict to serving God and his people with love and in spirit and truth. She is now an Evangelist and works with the help and jail ministry at her Church. I along with her family and friends truly thank God for keeping her and using her for His Kingdom.

-Sabrina Durr

Acknowledgements

Thank you to everyone who gave encouraging words and motivated me to keep pushing toward what God is trying to birth for his people.

Thank you to My Purpose and Confidence Coach Tia Crockett. You are truly God sent. You have helped me in many areas of my life and pulled things out of people that they are afraid to birth.

She is the dopest, she knows her purpose and helps others know theirs.

You are an amazing coach and author. You taught me the process of writing a book and made sure I didn't slack off from writing. Thank you, Coach Crockett! Love you.

Thank you to jCr3w Designs and Mimetes Edit Inc. for your contributions to my book. You gave my concepts life and served with much grace.